GREEN ALLEGIANTS

AND THE SECRET OF THE POISON GARDEN

ANANDA
THUMRUGOTI

First published by NU VOICE PRESS 2025
An imprint of Hubhawks Pvt. Ltd
www.nuvoicepress.com

This is a work of fiction and all characters and incidents described in this book are the product of the author's imagination. Any resemblance to actual persons, living or dead, is entirely coincidental.

ISBN: 978-81-987421-2-4.

Design & Typeset by
RBC WORLDWIDE, INDIA
www.rbcworldwide.com

Printed at Thomson Press
Published by Nu Voice Press

For Manonmani,
who loves a good story

Foreword

Every once in a while, a story comes along that surprises you—not with noise, but with quiet beauty. Green Allegiants is one such book. It reminded me of the joy of walking barefoot on damp earth, the quiet conversations you can have with trees, and the questions that only nature seems to answer.

This book is not just a thrilling mystery; it is a celebration of botanical intelligence and the quiet strength that can be found in the natural world.

I was drawn immediately into Durga Varma's world—not just because of the engaging plot, but because the story pulses with something rare in modern storytelling: reverence for the living green. As someone deeply invested in sustainable living and mindful science, I was struck by the originality of this narrative.

It is not often that we see young adult fiction woven so elegantly with plant lore, indigenous knowledge, and ecological inquiry. Ananda's writing reminds us that plants are more than background scenery—they are characters, teachers, and even silent witnesses to human choices. What stands out most is how the book brings together Indian heritage, knowledge of plant-based medicine, and empathy. Through the journeys of Durga and her friends, young readers are introduced to a world where curiosity is revered and where asking questions—about soil, seeds, or oneself—is a sign of courage.

I believe this is what makes Green Allegiants so important. It inspires children not just to learn but to observe. To listen. To care.

If you're holding this book in your hands, I hope you savour it. And I hope it plants something lasting in your imagination—because that, to me, is the true magic of reading!

— Uma Chigurupati

Executive Director of Granules India, Founder of Krsma Wines, Guinness World Record–holding marathoner, certified sommelier, and a passionate advocate of nature, sustainability, and mindful living.

Contents

1. A Dead Body on the School Grounds 9
2. Plantdemic! 22
3. The Coronation 35
4. Startling Revelations 48
5. A Disaster and An Opportunity 59
6. A New Discovery 71
7. Too Many Letdown Moments 84
8. Making the Most of Detention 99
9. Dead Body No. 2 112
10. Murder Mystery Deepens 125
11. Herb Garden Triggers a Thought 136

12. Adrian Picks up the Scent 148

13. An Unusual Clue, An Unusual Treasure 156

14. A Victory, Finally! 169

15. Tapping the Clues in Germany 182

16. A Time of Trial 195

17. The Forbidden Trail 205

18. The World Within 217

19. Much More Than Meets the Eye! 228

20. The Secret of the Poison Garden 238

21. Green Allegiants 253

Acknowledgments 270

About the Author 271

Green Allegiants...

Chapter One

A Dead Body on the School Grounds

"Name the plant."

My mind is fogging up...my tongue is parched. Where is that water? What was that question again? I...I...

Durga looked up and gulped nervously. Beads of sweat trickled down her forehead. Her quizzing team from Magnolia International School turned to look at her expectantly. *Them and the entire auditorium. Why are they staring at me like that? Why can't they leave me alone?* Durga thought unhappily. Her mind blanked out completely.

The tall, well-dressed, charismatic man with curly hair and Gandhi spectacles, Pratik Jain, Quiz Master, was quite well-known for introducing one unusual question round on plants. He stood on the stage, *expressionless*.

A tiny blip. The hall went utterly quiet. Pratik Jain turned to the other team.

"The Question passes to Team B."

Team B from St. Patricks was putting up a good fight. The smiling boy with spiky hair stood up.

That superior smirk. Durga's blood boiled.

"Botanical name is Mallotus rhamnifolius. Family, Euphorbiaceae, same as the Castor family."

"Correct answer," thundered Pratik Jain, and the hall erupted.

Oh yes! I know it better than that, bum! Buckthorn-leaved Kamala - a tree that grows 5m tall with greyish bark punctuated by warts, and round, velvety branchlets. Unisexual flowers. Wait, there's more. Buckthorn-leaved Kamala is usually found in peninsular India, in the Western Ghats - south of the Sahyadris, Sri Lanka and...

"And that brings us to the end of the final round…" Pratik was announcing the winners.

The hall emptied out within minutes. A desolate Team Magnolia stumbled out of the arena. Many of them were giving Durga a *still-can't-believe-a-geek-like-you-lost* look. Durga went pink.

"Diggy, c'mon, let's goooo," Janice Chandrasekhar, her best friend, was tugging at her sleeve. Janice was the daughter of Dr. Kennedy Chandrasekhar, her father's best friend and colleague of twenty years.

"I panicked, Jen. You know, when I get nervous, I get

flustered, and my hands get clammy. I feel I have a black hole instead of a brain! I simply cannot function under pressure," Durga moaned despairingly, as she walked out.

"*Arre, chal chhod na?* It's only a quiz. *Aasmaan tho girnewala nahi hai!*" Janice reverted to Hindi-Urdu whenever she felt muddled, thanks to her Hyderabadi upbringing. Durga smiled bleakly.

I am no good at Botany. I can't speak in public. How in the world can I make this clear to all? A volcano-sized guilt pang was wrenching her insides. Durga let out a really long sigh.

"Hey! Shall we head out to the cafeteria?" suggested Janice, eager to cheer up her bestie. Durga nodded.

Durga was nearly 11 and just didn't look it. She was the quiet one. No one knew much about her. She kept it that way. Her diminutive stature and lackluster dressing managed to camouflage her classically good-looking features - large expressive eyes, heart-shaped face, and thick waist-length hair that she determinedly kept plaited in pigtails that usually stayed on her shoulder.

Born Peesapati Durgavathi Lalithasindhuri Gajendrapatiraju, Durga belonged to the royal clan of Vijayanagaram. Her parents, however, had decided to name her Durga Varma in the hope that she would remain less conspicuous. And she *was*. Dr. Harish Varma, Durga's father, was more keen about his work in Botany than his noble title. And he was famous worldwide. Durga's mother, Peesapati

Avantika Lakshmi Gajendrapatiraju, was a well-known lawyer until she gave up her profession to help Dr. Varma in his expeditions. Durga wished she could be more like her parents. But she was convinced she was of a 'different' type - *yoga-doing, book-reading, lonely (loner?), well, basically a very small group-person…not one of those…*

Durga's train of thought was interrupted as her friends gathered around. They were all sitting where they usually sat - next to a large flowering bush, sipping an iced fresh lemon soda with a dash of mint.

"D, don't worry. We still have the Quiz in Germany. Let's start preparing for it ASAP," said the soft-spoken Abhik Bannerjee, the Telugu-fluent Bengali. Abhik (Abhi to his friends) was a prodigy of sorts, excelling in almost everything. Everyone was in awe of him. Rumor had it that he even hyper-customized his robotic wheelchair using AI. This was a bit of a stretch even for Abhik though he didn't outright *deny* it. His friends knew this, of course. They also *knew* that he rather enjoyed the attention.

"I am compiling a lot of interesting stuff," he went on. "Do you know? A newly discovered fungi turns flies into zombies and devours them inside out while they are still alive for a few days. Isn't that something to think about?!"

"*Eww!* Gross! Where do you even get stuff like that?"

"In the bushes! Hiding, hiding, hiding. Well, what else can a bunch of dopey geeks do? Having lost so spectacularly?"

The sneering voice of Akanksha Raju made them all turn around angrily.

Akanksha was a certified school bully. The Instagram-hottie types — *always-look-at-me* swag and impeccable grades, made her a formidable opponent. Her father, Dhyaneshwara Raju, was a top-shot lawyer, and her mother, Soundarya, was a well-known socialite.

As usual, she had her besties around her — a tall, gawky Odisha boy, Jug short for Jagannath Mishra, who excelled in Math, and Elizabeth Waltham (Lizzy), an Anglo-Indian, shy girl exceptional in English and Science, from Visakhapatnam city.

"Whoa, whoa, whoa, whoa, whoa! Hold your guts, sugar candy! *awww*… ever dressed as one! Hear, hear from this gorgeous, empty-headed lady in pink skirts who didn't even qualify for the final round!" Janice drew herself up expansively and smiled sardonically before starting to circle Akanksha in a very Hollywood villain fashion.

Janice was always extremely dramatic. As Durga always said, her Bharatanatyam dance training had permanently affected her. Whatever she did, it was like doing *abhinaya*. Standing 5'3" tall and athletic-looking, she simply loved the attention. And dressing up. She was voted Miss Popular two times in a row, apparently not without reason.

Durga sighed discreetly.

"Janice the Menace. By the way, I am here to warn you that the lounge behind the school auditorium is out of bounds for you. It's forbidden for anyone to step in there except the School Committee. You know, my father *sits* on that Committee..." Akanksha looked around pompously, pausing for effect.

Janice ignored this. As did the others.

Notwithstanding, Akanksha continued, "Heard you pinheads are grouping there regularly nowadays in the name of preparations. Anyways, all that show is for nothing — we are way ahead of you."

"Yo! First, get your facts right. We cleared with Madam Principal Roy to use the lounge. So, you are preparing *aha*...Do tell, what is the name of the fungi that turns insects into zombies and eats them alive?" demanded Janice.

"What???" Taken aback by the question, Akanksha turned quickly to Jagannath and Elizabeth. They fumbled uneasily and hung their heads.

We all have it coming, kid, squawked Abhik's pet Nibbles, the very talented African Grey Parrot, reeling off Clint Eastwood's famous movie one-liners in a very human-like voice. Clearly, this was all Abhik's training. Janice chortled. No one else did. The whole drama was simply too riveting.

"One day, I will personally KILL that parrot! KILL," fumed Akanksha stomping her foot.

"Well, there is no need for violence. The fungi is called Strongwellsea tigrinae," reeled off Keith Myers, the fourth member of Durga's group who had just come around. Blonde-haired, blue-eyed 11-year-old German Keith had startling, head-turning looks. As if to prove a point, he dressed shabbily and worked twice as hard at getting better grades. His parents were habitat designers based out of Mumbai who took up large-scale assignments.

"That is seriously cool!" bluttered Elizabeth, giving Keith admiring looks.

Akanksha's face went ashen grey.

Quickly recovering her composure, Akanksha shrieked, "This show-off here proves nothing. Let's go, guys." Akanksha stormed out. Jagannath and Elizabeth glared at them and followed her.

Suddenly, they heard shouts and saw people running in the school's extensive gardens. Someone was saying, "A dead body! At the lotus pond! And that poor fellow Shiva, the garden assistant, looks like he's dying too!" Durga and her friends hurried towards the crowd, quickly milling near the lotus pond.

Under the large, gnarly banyan tree, a thickset man with blonde hair and a tailored suit lay sprawled on the grass awkwardly to one side. Shiva was lying beside a bed of purple flowers, foaming at the mouth.

"Wow, this-this is too-" Janice never finished her

sentence. She gaped as Durga tore across, pushing people away roughly and reaching Shiva, ignoring the body. Janice followed. But instead of checking on Shiva, Durga knelt down to examine the purple flowers next to him. The perplexed crowd watched, fascinated. It was a unique occasion.

Just then, Professor Lata Anantanarayan, the Head of Life Sciences, reached the spot. *Uh-oh*…the crowd let out a disappointed groan as the teacher started making ferocious eyes at them.

Durga stood up calmly and said, "These purple flowers are Aconitum napellus, and they are extremely poisonous. This man may have touched them by mistake. And Shiva as well. If not treated quickly, he could also die very soon." The crowd went, *oooooh.* Professor Anantanarayan groaned aloud.

Just then, a wailing ambulance came to a brisk halt. Right behind was a police van. A physician hurried towards the two figures. Wrenching out his scope, he examined the sprawled figure for any sign of life. He shook his head and turned towards Shiva. Professor Anantanayaran stood next to him, talking animatedly. Finally, he stood up and said, "It does look like Aconitum flowers poisoning. We can save the boy."

The crowd stood transfixed as the stretchers got hauled into the ambulance. By now, Principal Roy, accompanied by the school's administrative staff, had also reached. She spoke briefly to the doctor, and the ambulance raced off.

"Unfortunately, the person who died is Dr. Uwe Schmitt, from the University of Cologne, Germany. He was here in the city on official business. He was to deliver a lecture at our school. Shiva will undergo treatment. I advise you all not to post anything on your social media walls or discuss this in the classrooms. If so, strict action will be taken. This is now a police matter. An official statement will be made later on. Please check your school app for updates. Now please disperse from here," said Principal Roy in her usual, commanding voice. The students disbanded slowly, whispering to each other in low tones.

Principal Roy came towards Durga and said quietly, "Good work! You have saved a life today, Durga. I will make sure that these poisonous plants are pulled out at once." She gave a slight nod, turned, and left to join the waiting police squad.

"My mind is blown! YOU Diggy lady are a *chhupa rustom!* How come you lose a simple quiz, and yet... come up with this fantastic deduction! Yes, Jen, I agree with you! *Chhupa* — that she is — a hidden gem! Way to go, D," finished Keith admiringly.

Durga blushed.

"Let's go and get something to eat, guys! I am like Han-gry" Janice was doing the *abhinaya* with fierce eyes. Durga rolled her eyes.

"So what's Han-gry?"

"State of anger caused by lack of food!"

"Ahhhh, Abhi, you are an *avatar* of ChatGPT, man!"

Abhik gave a satisfied grin.

"OK, let's get that food."

Janice literally pushed them all towards the cafeteria, hardly noticing the manicured bed of blooming roses along the side. The school, an inspirational venture of their principal, Professor Sarada Dutta Roy — a well-known educationist — was founded barely five years ago. Only last year, Durga and her friends entered this school built on 100 lush acres, overlooking the Bay of Bengal beach at Chirala, 300 km south of Hyderabad city, the 400-year-old capital of the South Indian state of Telangana. Anyone who visited the school was mesmerized by the lazy, untouched sweep of open fields dotted with mango and coconut groves and the meandering rivulets teeming with water lilies in many colors. The school admitted students only from the 5th standard, which was strictly based on merit and a stringent entrance exam.

The hearty meal consisted of a sizeable pan-fried vegetable pizza with extra cheese, mozzarella bites, a large kale salad with crispy chickpeas, chicken nuggets and strawberry ice cream.

"Why was he killed, I wonder?"

"Gosh! Jenny, why would you say *killed?*" asked Keith incredulously.

"It's more exciting that way. That's why K.. *he-he!"*

chuckled Janice.

"Shame on you, Jen. Very perv!"

"C'mon, give me a break, D. This is the single most exciting thing! Anyway, I am quite certain it's not a suicide…not by a long shot!" snorted Janice.

"Well, it could be a massive heart failure, too!" said Abhik.

"Actually, Nanna, I mean Dad, says that severe Aconitum napellus poisoning can lead to a massive cardiac arrest. I noticed that the dead man had vomited a lot, and a few flowers were missing from the bed, which was a bit out of place," murmured Durga.

"Wow, that sounds very deep! Could it be murder?"

Sometimes the dead can be more useful than the living.

"SHUT UP, NIBBLES!"

Durga laughed. "Have to admit Nibbles is feral! She's sassy and savage when it comes to lines, all thanks to you, Abhi. But, how does she know to say the right line at the right time, I wonder?"

"I didn't teach her that, D!"

Nobody said anything for a spell.

"Guys, we are getting a short break of one week. I think to clear up the dead body mess, no doubt. Most parents would be having heart attacks just hearing this *na?*" said Janice, busily checking the updates on her school app.

"Hmm, it turns out — the man, Dr. Uwe, *did* die of a heart attack. At least, that's what Google reports are saying. Well, I will be off to Mumbai for a few days. What about you all?" asked Keith.

"Maybe Jenny and I will also go home to Hyderabad. Why don't you both join us? Bamma will be thrilled!" Bamma was Durga's grandmother and also the Queen Mother.

"Hmm, that is a good idea. I will check with my parents and get back. What about you, Abhi?"

"Yup. Let me think about it," said Abhik.

Abhik's parents were well-known surgeons and were super-busy most of the time. Abhik loved spending time at the school, which was pet-friendly and had impressive architecture to support the specially-abled. Abhik loved getting around on his own instead of being escorted. This was the reason he avoided spending time elsewhere.

"By the way, *tada...*"

Janice was flaunting something that looked like an old leather pouch.

"What is it, Jen?"

"The mobile phone of the deceased! When you were kneeling to look at those flowers, I saw it lying in the grass and purloined it!"

"Pur-purloined...but why would you do something stupid like that?!!"

"It's exciting. Is-why! Who knows? We could get some clues," Janice's eyes were shining like diamonds.

"ARE YOU MAD??? THIS IS AGAINST THE LAW! WE COULD GO TO PRISON! STEALING THINGS AND THAT TOO FROM DEAD PEOPLE!"

"Oh shut up, D, do keep your voice down! I now realize it's a m-mistake now. Let me figure out how to return it. But first things first, let's check his messages."

Even before Durga could say anything else, Janice had already figured out the passcode to open the phone and was frantically checking the WhatsApp messages on it.

"Heyo, D, here's a message to your dad!!"

"WHAT???"

Durga snatched the phone.

"What is it?" asked Keith excitedly

"Two days from now. They will plan it. Please make the arrangements. And Nanna replied, *Sure. Rest assured. I will not let it happen.* There is a Google location too. That's-that's in Hyderabad. Wow, that's pretty close to home. But it's only a horticultural show. What could be there? How very mysterious!"

"This is too exciting to miss. We are all coming to Hyderabad, D," chorused Keith, Abhik, and Janice.

Durga grinned.

Chapter Two

Plantdemic!

Durga was lounging in a comfortable settee facing the window, her head buried in a voluminous Space Encyclopaedia. She was also waiting for her friends to arrive. Try, as she did, her mind wandered back to the message. Her parents were out for an official engagement when she arrived home the previous evening. There was no time to talk.

"I can't believe Uwe is dead! He wanted to meet us. It's getting tricky, Kenny. This proves only one thing: that we are right! They must have sensed that we were getting too close. In any case, I plan to be at the location tonight. You take care. Call me once you land."

Startled, Durga turned around to see her father, Dr. Harish Varma, who had just walked in, speaking on the phone. He hadn't noticed her.

With his salt and pepper hair, Dr. Varma was fit and handsome in a nerdy sort of way. Only recently, he was anointed the King of the erstwhile Kingdom of Vijayanagaram by his Grandfather Rajasaheb Peesapati Sarath Chandronmaya Sivendra Gajendrapatiraju, who had adopted him in order to make him the royal heir. He was now H.E. Peesapati Harishchandra Bhoopala Gajendrapatiraju.

In the modern-day republic, the coronation was only symbolic, as the royal family did not hold any positions of power to run the state or collect taxes. However, Durga's family was wealthy, owned assets, and was the custodian of several palaces and much artwork.

Despite his coronation, Dr. Harish Varma decided to keep his non-royal title and continue his scientific research. His work, particularly in unearthing the lost indigenous varieties of plants, was considered valuable by scholars worldwide.

"Are you talking to Uncle Kenny, Nanna? What is it about?" asked Durga.

Dr. Varma turned around hastily.

"Oh, you are here?! I didn't see you. Well, we are discussing plant theft. Uwe, the one who unfortunately died on your school campus, was hot on the trail of some miscreants. Kenny and I were helping him find them..."

"Oh, Nanna, then did you get that message…I mean…" Durga was about to ask him when her mother walked in, saying "Can we have breakfast? It's already 8:30 AM!"

Lakshmi had given up her thriving legal profession a few years ago to help Dr. Varma in his expeditions. Durga wished she could be like her—*fearless*.

"Yes, Lakshmi, let's. I am hungry. Come Amma, Durga, join us please."

Durga put her book down and joined them.

"So, how did Dr. Uwe die?" asked Durga's mother inquiringly, putting down her teacup.

The light streaming in from two large French windows illuminated the morning room done up entirely in pale blue. The seventeenth-century oak table had many delicious dishes, fresh juices, salads, and sweets. Adit, their butler, stood one pace behind Dr. Varma's chair, ready to serve.

"Durga… tell your mom."

"Well, Amma. He died due to a massive cardiac arrest. It was I who found him among the Aconitum shrubs. It could have been Aconitum poisoning. Right, Nanna?"

"Oh, my God!" exclaimed Lakshmi, turning to look at Durga, with a worried expression.

"Oh, I wasn't alone, Amma," assured Durga.

"Yes. it's very much possible," replied Dr. Varma. "Jenny told me. About that Acontinum poisoning deduction and saving Shiva. Impressive, Durga!"

Thank God. He didn't say anything about the quiz. Durga heaved a sigh of relief.

"It comes to you naturally!" Dr. Varma smiled.

Durga managed a smile.

"Well, there is more news today. Durga...go on."

It took her only a few moments to figure out why. *Oh yeah, the lotus!*

"Yup Nanna, I just read it in the newspaper. Nymphaea thermarum, the smallest water lily in the world has been stolen!"

"I am glad you are keeping yourself updated, Durga," smiled Dr. Varma appreciatively.

"Well, what about it?" asked Lakshmi curiously, removing her glasses and polishing them absently with her saree *pallu*.

"You know, it would have become nearly extinct if not for the efforts of Spanish scientific horticulturist Carlos Magdalena, who recreated the conditions of a hot spring by heating mud so that the plant survived. And now it is stolen! From London's Botanical Gardens! It seems lotuses are not a priority for the Crime Units, so they closed the case in 10 days. Plant theft is not a priority in any part of the world. I am sure there is organized crime behind this. It's no longer a simple affair. In fact, they are calling it the Plantdemic! As this is happening more and more after the pandemic."

Who cares for plants and botany, really? Durga sighed. *Space, on the other hand, offers limitless possibilities...*

"What would actually happen if they steal plants, Hari?" asked Lakshmi.

"Well, as a botanist, I would say biodiversity is key to our very existence. Some rare plants could contain wonder drugs that cure deadly diseases. That's why they are invaluable." explained Dr. Varma.

Lakshmi nodded.

Durga shrugged and silently went back to her book.

"Let's resume our botanical expedition this week, Lakshmi. Kenny will not be able to join. He is traveling to Cambridge for that lecture."

Kenny was Janice's father, Dr. Kennedy Chandrasekhar.

"You are off again, Nanna? Is Amma going with you ?" asked Durga anxiously.

"Yes, sweetie. You can join if you want!" said her father.

"I can't, Nanna, and I will miss you both. My friends may turn up, and I want to stay with Bamma."

"That's okay. You can join me in my next expedition."

Durga's mum came and kissed her on the cheek. Durga waved as her parents left to pack.

Durga's house was a mansion of sorts. Hyderabadis called it a Devdi. It was a part of her family's princely legacy. It had a Grand Hall, many rooms, an elaborate courtyard, and a garage filled with many cars, both vintage and the latest models. Her room overlooked a manicured green lawn with a large, sculpted bronze fountain.

A loud thumping on the stairs was followed by several loud '*oohs*' and '*aahs,*' and Janice staggered into the room, panting. Durga grinned. There was always drama when Janice was in the picture.

"Okie Jen, what is it this time?"

"What is it? What is it? The whole world is collapsing. It's Armageddon, lady — the end of the world. That's what it is!"

"No..."

"Don't tell me you haven't heard?" exclaimed Janice, waving her arms expressively.

"What is it that I was supposed to have heard?"

"Well, you know what our Ms-Nose-up-in-the-air did?"

"WILL YOU GET TO THE POINT???"

"Okie, okie. Akku, aka Akanksha, is contesting for the Cultural Secretary post. If she does, we are finished!!"

Magnolia had four House Teams named after famous Indian scientists: CV Raman, APJ Abdul Kalam, MS Swaminathan, and Mokshagundam Visveswarayya. All the students were sorted into these four. Throughout the year, the Houses collected points on various accounts such as good behavior, merit, and talent. The one among the four with the highest score was awarded the House Cup at the end of the year. Durga and her friends were in APJ Abdul Kalam House, while Akanksha and her friends were in CV Raman house, which made them bitter rivals.

"Oh, this is a disaster! Who is contesting against her from APJ?"

"Not anyone so far, Diggy. No one dares to. It looks like she will sail through. You know who is overseeing this, Professor Vishal Bharadwaj."

Suddenly, Janice sat up. "I got the most fantastic idea in the whole wide world!"

Durga's eyebrows shot up.

"The only solution for this is Diggy if YOU can contest!"

"WHAT?? ME?? HAVE YOU GONE COMPLETELY NUTS???"

"Well, you know you've got it in you. You have grades and fancy; after all, you are a royal, your father is such a well-known scientist, and if we can spruce you up a bit, you will be ready," Janice was looking hopefully at Durga.

"NO. NO. NO. Why don't YOU take it up? You are the Ms. Popular, whatever, and have a bigger circle of friends."

"Nah... Your grades are way, way better, you sing like a nightingale, and you DO have that 'arty look.' People may like the contrast," finished Janice.

Durga sat stunned. Never in her wildest dreams would she contemplate any such thing. She just wanted to remain as invisible as possible.

"It's time we, I mean YOU, take up a leadership role, Diggy. It will give us a chance to do our thing — like introduce better picnics and excursions, have Netflix in the common room..." Janice's voice took a dreamier turn.

"HEYYY!!! IS THIS WHY I SHOULD TAKE UP THIS...FOR THIS LOONY BIN SCHEME OF YOURS???"

"Uh-huh, Diggy, sorry. I-I meant important stuff you like — helping underprivileged students, debating groups, bringing new books into our outdated library, more recreational hours... If SHE comes, you know she will just throw meaningless parties or fool around, but YOU, on the other hand..." Janice changed her tactics instantly.

"Oh, that could make sense, I suppose," said Durga, still looking most unconvinced.

"Thank you, Diggy!!!" screamed Janice, kissing her on the cheek. Durga smiled.

Both were silent for a spell. Janice's eyes settled on the *Times of India*. Languidly, she picked it up and screamed.

"Heyo D! The Rose Show! It's today! Remember the location? The message?"

"Oh yes! I completely forgot! Shoot! I wanted to ask my dad if he wanted to be there, but my parents have already started. By the way, when are Abhi and Keith coming?"

Wake me up if we crash into the mountain. I wouldn't want to miss that.

Durga and Janice froze for one second.

"Nibbles," grinned Janice as they raced towards the door to see Keith and Abhik enter.

"So glad you guys could join us."

"Who can say no to you, Your Highness," said Keith, making a lavish mock bow. Abhik grinned.

"*Eww*. Stop that! Jeez, am I happy to see you all here!"

Just then, Durga's grandmother walked in.

Peesapati Jyotirmayi Aradhya Lakshmi Gajendrapatiraju, looked regal, with her thick, lustrous hair fading into a dignified grey twisted into a severe chignon. But nothing could restrain the silvery curls that circled her serene face with large eyes and a prominent nose on which shimmered a small diamond, giving her a natural poise. She wore a pastel-shade Uppada handloom saree with a matching Cashmere shawl draped gracefully around her shoulders and no other jewelry.

"Namaskaram Bamma," they all chorused. Being childhood friends, they always called her Bamma, just as Durga did.

"Blessings to you. I'm very glad you all are together

again. That will cheer us all up. Let's have lunch on the terrace. Boys, you can settle into the same rooms as last time. What are your plans for today?"

"Bamma, we want to attend the Rose Show at Nampally Public Gardens. Will Amma and Nanna come there?" asked Durga

"Oh! I don't know about that. They might not, considering they have a long drive ahead of them.Meanwhile, I will have Mr. Krishna Murthy, our Estate Manager escort you all, " she said, leaving the room.

The Rose Show was beautiful, with arrays of colorful roses blooming merrily along carefully planned pathways. Durga, Janice, Abhik, and Keith stood there mesmerized. An enthusiastic crowd had gathered to admire the Rose Show, hosting over 2000 varieties of roses of different colors and shades spread across the famous Jubilee Hall in Public Gardens. On the Queen Mother's suggestion, they met Mrs. Rekha Shyam, the President of the Hyderabad Rose Society.

"The Hyderabad Rose Society is one of the oldest environmentalist societies of the twin cities of Hyderabad and was founded nearly four decades ago. This time, we are showing some exceptionally rare varieties, such as Gold Medal Rose and Michelangelo Rose. Our star attraction this time is the World's rarest rose — Juliet Rose. It was with great difficulty that we managed to get the rose for display here. It costs 5 million dollars, and is a security nightmare!

Why don't you check it out before the crowds grow?" advised Mrs. Rekha Shyam, also an Ikebana Maestro.

Around the corner was a highly guarded pavilion. They were quickly escorted in once Mr. Krishna Murthy spoke to the organizing team. On an exquisitely crafted pavilion sat a vase that presented the Juliet Rose.

"Super!"

"Lovely!"

"Yes. The Juliet Rose is considered one of the rarest flowers in the world because it took 15 years for rose breeder David Austin to cultivate the flower in England," explained Mrs. Rekha.

The Juliet Rose was entrancing. The full-cupped rose with distinctive petals was an apricot color with a pleasing fragrance. The entire shrub was about 3.5 to 4 feet tall, with numerous blooms.

"I can look at it for an eternity," sighed Janice.

"Yes, Jen, that's why it's been named Juliet, inspired by the Shakespearean classic — Romeo and Juliet. " said Abhik

"Wow! What's that?" asked Janice, pointing towards another beautiful rose that had bright petals in a creamy shade of butter yellow.

"That is the Michelangelo rose, Jenny. It is usually quite big in size, as you can see," explained Durga distractedly. She tried calling her parents, but their mobiles were out of reach.

They stepped out, savoring the aromatic fragrance that hung in the air. Suddenly, Abhik motioned to them to be quiet, pointing towards the Juliet Rose pavilion. Durga, Keith, and Janice turned around to see security personnel rushing about, looking tense.

Mrs. Rekha Shyam and Mr. Krishna Murthy were busy talking and didn't notice anything.

Just as Janice was about to speak, Abhik made the 'do-not-speak' gesture that made her clam up. He unwrapped his high-resolution telescopic camera lens (which was incredibly small to be noticed), and pointed it towards the Juliet Rose pavilion. Within minutes, he put it down, and they all huddled together to hear what he had to say.

"It's stolen!"

"What???"

"The Juliet Rose plant."

"You must be kidding!"

"No, my laser-hand telescopic camera sees everything. The plant has been stolen!"

Within seconds, Durga had jogged up to the pavilion only to be stopped from entering, by the stern security personnel.

"It's true then," said Durga, trotting back. "They won't let me inside. Why would they not let me inside if the plant hadn't been stolen?"

"Wow, D, so it's true!"

That message! It's true. But why did dad not do anything about it, wondered Durga. A feeling of unease filled her almost instantly.

They started walking.

"D, please don't panic," said Abhik in the lowest of his voices, handing over his mobile to her as she turned around.

"I just saw the news on Google. Your parents met with an accident."

Janice grabbed it from Durga and read it aloud.

'World-renowned Botanist Dr. Harish Varma and his wife injured in a massive accident!'

Dr. Harish Varma (45), accompanied by his wife, Mrs. Peesapati Avantika Lakshmi Gajendrapatiraju (40), were traveling by car when this disaster occurred. Both of them have been admitted to a well-known corporate hospital in Hyderabad.

"My God!"

Durga staggered and fainted.

Chapter Three

The Coronation

As Durga came around, she saw the kindly face of the lady doctor peering at her. All her friends were standing around her. They were back at the Devdi. Queen Mother was sitting next to the bed. Durga tried to get up, but Janice ran to her side and made her lie down again.

"Durga, Amma, and Nanna are receiving treatment. Don't panic," assured her grandmother soothingly. After a few moments, she left them to talk to Mr. Krishna Murthy.

Janice looked at Durga worriedly. She had a strange expression on her face.

"Diggy, just talk to me. What are you thinking?"

"The accident, theft at Rose Show, Dr. Uwe's death — it's getting deadlier. In fact, dad told me this morning that he, along with Uncle Kenny and Dr. Uwe, were hot on the trail of the gang responsible for this."

Abhik, Keith, and Janice nodded.

"Now, wait a minute! I still have the mobile phone of the chap who died. We could hand it over to the police and explain everything," cried Janice as she rushed towards her room to get the mobile.

Within minutes, she was back, panting.

"Oh god, guys, the mobile phone...it's gone!!!"

"What?? Have you checked properly?" chorused Keith, Abhik, and Durga.

"Yes. I had left it in my room!"

"What??!! Theft at our Devdi? That is just impossible!" exclaimed Durga breathlessly.

"This brings up another issue. The more important one. Someone is spying on us!" whispered Abhik.

"And...going through our things!!!" finished Keith.

"But why? What do we do now?"

Everyone fell silent.

"Maybe we should spy back," suggested Abhik.

"Spy on whom?" asked Jenny.

"Well, I can install spy devices outside our rooms and keep a watch. I am sure we will find the culprit in no time!"

Durga nodded.

A knock on the door made them sit up. Queen Mother

entered the room and went to sit near Durga. Cradling her head in her arms, she started speaking.

"Don't worry, Talli. Amma and Nanna are undergoing treatment. Your mother is better; however, your father may have some issues..."

"What issues, Bamma?" implored Durga.

"His memory. Doctors say it could be because of the accident trauma. Let's pray that everything turns out okay. They will come back home by tomorrow."

Lunch followed. But no one was in any mood to enjoy the delicious spread.

After lunch, they walked towards the garden to get some air.

"Abhi, let's install those spycams to check who's spying on us."

"Sure, D, let's get back then."

It took only a few minutes for Abhik to install tiny devices at vantage points.

"Now what?" asked Keith

"We wait!"

They tried various ways to cheer themselves up with books, playing carroms, and video games.

Nibbles dozed.

One hour later…

"Guys, I see some action," whispered Abhik.

"I can vaguely see a man entering your room, D!" said Abhik, zooming in on the image. Slowly, the image became more precise.

Durga watched spellbound! It was Mr. Krishna Murthy! Their estate manager!

"What in the world! How dare he?"

"But what is he searching for, D?" asked Jenny.

"I don't know Abhi. Please zoom in further. He's carrying something in his hands."

"Yes, D. He's carrying your school journal!"

"Well, there is nothing in it."

"Why would he do that?"

"Well, we must keep watching!"

Durga was standing near the window in her room when she heard a gentle knock. Her grandmother came in. Wordlessly, they both walked towards the elaborate loungers arranged in her room.

Queen Mother took Durga's hands into hers. Durga

looked deeply into her grandmother's eyes.

Her grandmother seemed unnaturally calm. *She was always like that!*

"Amma, Durga, if we let sadness and pain settle in our hearts, one day, it will overwhelm us. Being courageous is something we need to cultivate on a day-to-day basis."

Durga nodded silently.

"I know, Bamma. I am trying very hard."

"You have to try harder, my dear. As the heir to the Throne, you must strive to become an inspiration like your father."

"Heir? To the Throne?"

"The Throne cannot be vacant. Tradition decrees that we anoint you to take the place of your father."

Durga stood astonished.

Bamma, I am not capable. I am not a leader. I am a coward.

"I don't want it, Bamma. Father will be back, then what? Are these old traditions still followed in this age and time?" cried Durga.

"Yes, you will retain your title even when your father returns. But in the meantime, you have to take his place. None of us can."

"Bamma, tell me more about our family."

"We belong to the royal clan of Kshatriyas of the Suryavanshi sect. Our ancestors were very progressive and well-versed in music and the science of Ayurveda. Your grandfather, His Highness Rajasaheb Peesapati Sarath Chandronmaya Sivendra Gajendrapatiraju, was the King at the time. Rajasaheb, was instrumental in adopting and anointing Hari, your father, who was related to us, to be the King," paused Queen Mother.

"Oh, okay. But there are no kings anymore in India. Right?"

"Yes. In independent India, kingdoms have ceased to exist. However, you will be the head of an ancient clan. Our town folk and community still seek our support to solve their issues. You will do the same in the future."

Durga nodded.

"Well, let me tell you a little more about the process. You will sit on a throne and be anointed as the Princess, which is quite a formal process. Your coronation ceremony is tomorrow. Considering the circumstances, we have invited only a small gathering, and no media will be present. That means no social media posts either."

Durga was taken aback but said nothing.

"Our dynasty is very ancient, Durga, and we hold the key to many secrets..."

“Secrets? Of what sort, Bamma?”

“You will automatically know. Our Court Astrologer, Meenakshi Amma insisted that we complete the ceremony tomorrow.”

“But how can I do this without Amma and Nanna? Won’t they feel bad?” asked Durga tearfully.

Queen Mother held up Durga’s chin and, looking directly into her eyes, said, “They know the rules. They will understand. We must be watchful, Talli. We do have enemies. Some are ancient, and some are recent. I believe they are constantly at work to destabilize us. We must be prepared.”

Durga sighed as her grandmother left the room.

The large pavilion in the house, the Hamsa Mandapam, could seat at least 1000 guests. It was shaped like a swan and decorated elaborately with garlands of fresh flowers and green mango leaves. A silver throne studded with many precious stones was placed facing the East. A large, life-size portrait of Rajasaheb Peesapati Sarath Chandronmaya Sivendra Gajendrapatiraju hung on the wall. Queen Mother sat on a resplendent throne next to the raised platform. Fourteen royal priests sat on the right-hand side of the platform.

For Durga, it was all too ostentatious. As she turned around to see, her grandmother caught her eye and nodded. Durga was dressed in a traditional Kanchivaram saree. She wore her mother's necklace called Kanthi, set in Burma rubies and diamonds in five alternating tiers. On her feet were golden anklets set in diamonds. Janice too, was dressed in an elaborate saree and adorned with ornaments. Keith and Abhik were presented with traditional but tailored Indian suits and made to sit near the Throne.

Durga was woken up early, around 2:30 AM. After a brief ceremony at the Ganesha temple on the premises, she was escorted to the Hamsa Mandapam. As the clock struck 5:00, a host of dignitaries started arriving. Among them were Cabinet-rank Ministers, Chief Ministers, bureaucrats, important state dignitaries, and old family friends of the Gajendrapatiraju dynasty.

The ceremony began precisely at 5:15 AM, and ended one hour later. A bejeweled sword was handed over to her as Queen Mother placed a crown set in sapphires, emeralds, pearls, and jade on Durga's head. A large diamond ring was slipped on her right ring finger.

As Durga bent down to touch her grandmother's feet, the Queen Mother quickly caught her midway, looked full into her eyes, and said, "My dear, you bow to no one. You are the Princess of Vijayanagaram, the scion of the proud Gajendrapatirajus. Always hold your head high and rule wisely."

The coronation ceremony and an elaborate breakfast later, the guests left by 8:00 AM. Durga, Janice, Abhik, and Keith returned to their room, discarded their elaborate costumes, slipped into comfortable denims, and escaped to the garden.

They all sat on a bench under a great, big banyan tree. Even Nibbles was quiet for a change.

"I am longing for a cheeseburger," exclaimed Janice. All of them thumbs upped in agreement.

They all walked into the large, sophisticated-looking kitchen with state-of-the-art cooking appliances and a kindly chef.

"Do you think we could have something light like a cheeseburger or cake?" asked Durga.

And strawberries, please squealed Nibbles.

The Chef smiled and requested them all to be seated.

He did a better job than they expected. They enjoyed a delicious meal consisting of cheeseburgers, a tossed salad, chocolate donuts, and an ice cream featuring fresh strawberries.

"This is delish," exclaimed Keith as they all dug in hungrily.

Super, Super! squealed Nibbles.

After the meal, they all returned to their rooms to rest.

Once in her room, Durga found she was too restless to nap. There was still no news of her parents, only that they were stable. The large, sculpted box with the sword was on the table.

The box was beautifully carved in fragrant sandalwood and bore many Indian motifs. She opened it to see the bejeweled sword lying on a blue velvet cloth. A small inlay card had all the details. The blade was made of Wootz steel or ukku, famously smelted in Telangana. The technique of smelting Wootz steel was considered unique but was lost entirely by the mid-nineteenth century with the conquest of the British.

Slowly, Durga unsheathed the sword that had a golden hilt inlaid with diamonds, rubies, and emeralds. The fine blade shone and sparkled in the afternoon light, filling Durga with pride. The razor-sharp blade was inscribed and bore verses from the Bhagavad Gita. The wooden sheath was covered with maroon velvet. Behind the sheath was a small leather clip that helped fasten it to one's belt.

As she examined the precious gems and stones, a small panel swung open noiselessly! Astonished, she put her fingers inside and found a small, folded parchment. She cautiously brought it out. The parchment was made of thick raw silk, now faded with age. Carefully, she opened the folds. It was a graphical design. She got her magnifying glass to look at it carefully.

She realized it was a classic Pattachitra painting from Odisha with fine and minute details. In the middle was a temple atop a mountain. Vaguely, she could see that the deity in the temple was Shiva; she could also make out a creek, a forest, and some caves. In the background was a waterbody. There was also a very elaborate map marked in Sanskrit.

There were two slokas to the right, and left.

She enhanced the image on the right.

trai-vidyā māṁ soma-pāḥ pūta-pāpā

yajñair iṣhṭvā svar-gatiṁ prārthayante

te puṇyam āsādya surendra-lokam

aśhnanti divyān divi deva-bhogān

She googled and found the sloka from the Bhagavad Gita, Chapter 9, Verse 20, with meaning.

People who find pleasure in the practices mentioned in the Vedas worship Vishnu. They partake in the Soma juice, which is the leftover from yajñas, to cleanse themselves of sin and aspire to reach heaven. Through their virtuous actions, they are able to enter the realm of Indra, the ruler of heaven, where they experience the delights of the divine beings.

The one on the left was:

Yattadagre vishameva parinaamemritopapam
tatsukham saattvikam proktamaatmabuddhiprasaadajam

This was also from Bhagavad Gita, Chapter 18, Verse 18.

The translation was thus -

That which is like poison initially but is like nectar in its result, that joy is said to be saatvic, born of one's mental purity.

Soma? Was this some sort of a secret? she wondered.

She took a pic of the scroll, set aside the sword, and started studying the patterns on the floor of the box.

There were lots of carvings. Carefully, she traced her fingers along the carving, and once again, the floor slid open noiselessly, revealing another chamber below.

Right in the middle, laid on a red velvet cloth, was a small bunch of copper plates in the chamber secured by a big, circular copper seal with the royal emblem of the Gajendrapatirajus. The legend around the emblem proclaimed in Sanskrit, *Hail, Prosperity!* The seal itself was a work of art. It had an elephant, the emblem of the Gajendrapatirajus, an umbrella, a swastika, and two lamps, all auspicious symbols. Durga tentatively tried to open it but realized it was sealed with a thick metallic band.

Next to it were rows of labeled glass jars filled with some dried plant material. Next to the glass jars, there was a thick-set journal. Durga intuitively knew it was her father's because of the handwriting.

A knock at her door brought Durga back, and she raced to open it. Janice, Abhik, and Keith came in. She closed the door.

"Guys, you need to see this!"

Chapter Four

Startling Revelations

"This is too amazing!"

Janice, Abhik, and Keith circled the box in utter admiration.

Durga picked up the copper plates bunch and laid them on the table.

"I can see the verses on the top of the emblem here. This is in Sanskrit.

Hita hitam sukham dukham ayus tasaya hitahitam!

Mana ch tachha yatrokatam ayurveda sa uchyate !!

I can read these verses. The footnote annotation says this sloka is from Charaka Samhita. In Sanskrit, Ayur means an ancient system of life, and Veda means knowledge. So that's Ayurveda," translated Keith.

"Wow, Keith, that's awesome!"

“Thanks, guys. Thanks to my mother, a scholar in Sanskrit,” Keith blushed modestly.

“But how to get them to open?” muttered Durga.

They tried various ways. Even after an hour, there was no progress. It was exasperating.

“Gosh, I want to sit,” exclaimed Janice, and they all plonked down on the soft carpet on the floor, except Keith, who kept inspecting the box. Nibbles sat on a perch, looking down contentedly.

“Let’s check these bottles. There are about ten here. The labels have both the Sanskrit name and its counterpart in English. This one says Guduchi or Tinospora cordifolia,” observed Keith, taking out a jar and reading the label.

Durga rushed towards the box and opened her father’s journal. Each page of the journal had a detailed drawing of various plants, their names in Sanskrit, and the corresponding names in English. There were also elaborate descriptions of each plant.

“My father’s journal has many references here! Wait, there are three columns here. One has the name of a raga, a number, and the name of a herb. Well, I know what these numbers mean. The numbers and the ragas are the same as they are Meḷakartas,” said Durga, reading the journal.

“What are those?” wondered Keith.

“Oh I could tell you that. Carnatic classical music has a

collection of fundamental ragas. They are 72 in number and are called Meḷakartas. Meḷakarta ragas are the parent ragas or Janaka ragas from which other ragas can be generated," explained Abhik.

"Wow, Abhi, did you ever learn music?" asked Janice.

"No, but I have been researching Indian music and its forms."

"And...we were playing video games," sighed Keith

"Okay, coming back. What is the connection between the ragas and the ingredients?" asked Janice.

"That's what we need to figure out," said Durga.

A knock on the door made them all turn around.

"Your Royal Highness Princess Durgavathi, tea is served on the terrace," announced a lady in a white and gold saree.

"Thank you, Pushpa. Guys, meet Pushpa. She has been taking care of me for the last few years," said Durga, introducing the lady, who bowed again.

Thank you. You can go now mimicked Nibbles in a human voice from the perch.

Pushpa looked confused, smiled at the parrot, and went away.

Janice giggled. "I say we can use Nibbles to play tricks on people."

All of them laughed.

"Let's take a tea break. I am kinda hungry," said Abhik.

The tea was sumptuous — creamy scones, tea cakes, pastries, freshly baked donuts, a selection of cut fruits, and milkshakes.

The view from the terrace garden was spectacular, offering a great view of the entire herb garden.

"This is delectable," said Abhik, enjoying the treats.

Nibbles regaled them all with entertaining mimicry of various sounds.

Durga was back in her room. Her mind was buzzing.

Just then, Janice, Keith, and Abhik came in.

They all stared at the copper plates.

"D, if these are ragas, there must be a connection between them and these copper plates. You sing and practice Carnatic music, don't you? Maybe...you should sing to it…" suggested Keith.

"Really??" said Durga incredulously.

"Well, why not? You have nothing to lose…Diggy."

"Yes, yes…let me see."

Durga opened the journal, checked the list, and found the number three written next to Ganamurthy raga.

"Okay, guys, here goes. I recently finished a few kirthanas in Meḷakarta ragas in my music class. I will sing *Ganamurthe Sri Krishna Venuganalola*, a kirthana composed by Saint-Poet Sri Tyagaraja. Please don't mind if there are any mistakes."

"That's unlikely since none of us know Carnatic music," exclaimed Keith.

Durga smiled, sat on her lounger, switched on the Tanpura droid on her mobile, checked her shruti, and sang the arohana and avarohana, the ascending and descending scale patterns of the raga, following it up with the kirthana.

The entire group sat mesmerized as Durga's mellifluous voice resonated across the room.

The minute Durga stopped, there was complete silence. Durga looked around uneasily at her friends, who seemed utterly dazed. And then the group came alive with resounding applause.

"You are a magician, Diggy!"

"Super singing. You have a sweet voice."

"Absolutely brill D!"

Nibbles made a fantastic applause mimicry.

Durga glowed. She never actually sang in front of others

except in her practice session.

"Okay, let's see if something happened," Durga walked over to the copper plates.

Janice, Keith, and Abhik followed.

"Guys! The copper plates are open!" Janice squealed and jumped.

"Correction Jenny. Only one has sprung out. It has some inscription on it,"

"Guys, let me read it," said Keith.

Durga snapped a pic of the plate, and Keith peered at the marking on the plate.

"Well, the letter on the top is number three in Sanskrit. Here, it is some recipe, a brew for improving sleep, memory, etc. The main herb is Ashwagandha."

"Let's now check my father's journal. Number three is Ashwagandha — scientific name Withania somnifera. The description says it is a small woody plant native to India and North Africa. Its root and berries are used to produce many ayurvedic remedies," finished Durga.

"Okay. What does that mean?" asked Janice.

Durga was silent for a few moments. Nobody said anything.

"The copper plates are filled with ayurvedic remedies. Each of the 72 Meḷakarta ragas unravels one plate with a remedy that is connected to a particular raga. My father may have been researching this," said Durga.

"Wow! Amazing, D!"

"Guys, I want to try another one. This time, let me check the journal for a herb and then connect it to a raga," said Durga, tracing the journal's list.

They all nodded.

"Let's try this: Lilium polypyllum, White lily in English, Kshirakakoli in Sanskrit, a 30-100 cm tall perennial herb that bears fragrant, white creamy flowers with purple dots. This species is found in Jammu-Kashmir, Himachal Pradesh, and Uttarakhand. The bulbs of the plant are underground and have medicinal properties. Its bulb works as an expectorant, astringent, antipyretic, and helps improve general debility. Which is why it is widely used in ayurvedic preparations. The number of the corresponding raga is 15, which is Mayamalavagowla. Let me try this."

They all settled comfortably and placed the copper plates on a small settee right in the middle.

Durga switched on the Tanpura droid and sang the arohana and avarohana.

"Yippee, another copper pate is open!!!" screamed Janice once again.

Keith translated the inscription.

"The Sanskrit inscription says to grind the Kshirakakoli

bulbs and drink it with water," translated Keith.

Durga went back to the chest.

"Here's the bottle with Lilium polypyllum bulbs. Cool!" said Durga, holding up the bottle.

"Super. Super. So, was Krishna Murthy trying to steal this journal?" Janice wondered.

"Not possible! How would he know about it?" wondered Durga

"Maybe he was looking for any details you may have noted down about Dr. Uwe," offered Abhik.

"Now, that's possible, I suppose."

"Hmm, let's wait and see," sighed Janice.

A mango milkshake later, they all settled on the terrace again and started playing a game of Scrabble. It was getting dark.

Just as they were finishing, Pushpa came in through the door.

"Your Highness Princess Durgavathi, your grandmother has requested your audience."

"Thank you, Pushpa. I will be there."

“Guys, give me some time,” said Durga, rising as she followed Pushpa through the long corridor to her Grandmother’s room.

Her Grandmother came forward to hug her. Pushpa left, closing the door behind them.

“Amma, would you like to come to the hospital? We can go now and be back by nightfall?”

Durga nodded eagerly.

“I will be downstairs in 10.”

Durga went to her room to change.

Her friends had gone back to their rooms.

Durga opened the box, inspected the herbs, took a small quantity of the Kshirakakoli herb, powdered it, and pocketed it.

She carefully replaced the ingredients, the copper plates, the journal, and the sword in the sculpted box. She then lifted the box and placed it in a large secret locker inside the cupboard behind a painting. She sealed the vault with a new password.

As she rushed downstairs, she punched a *Going to the hosp. Will be back soon.* WhatsApp message to her friends, and went to meet her Grandmother.

In a few minutes, they reached the hospital. As they entered the special room, Durga saw her mom and dad lying on beds, swathed in bandages. They looked peaceful. A team of doctors surrounded them. A sob broke in her throat as she rushed towards them and sat next to their beds. The Hospital's Medical Director, Dr. Mohammed Khan, requested that Queen Mother enter his office for a briefing. Together, they left the room.

As Durga sat holding their hands, tears welled up in her eyes. Soon, a nurse came in with a tray bearing glasses of orange juice. She checked the vitals and made notes. Her mobile vibrated, and she stepped out to take the call.

Durga seized the moment. Taking a deep breath, she slipped the herb powder into the glasses. Just then, her Grandmother came back into the room.

Durga spent a night of utter desolation. To fight it, she binge-watched a popular soap. Seeing her parents like that was a big shock for her. Finally, at around 4:00 AM, she fell into an exhausted sleep. Around 7:00 AM, she felt her grandmother's hands on her head, soothing her.

"Good news, amma. Your mother is well and almost normal. Your father is conscious and feeling much better, but his memory still seems to be a problem. Dr. Khan says it will get better. What is extraordinary is in just one night, some miracle has brought them back! May God be praised. Our good doctor says they can come back home tomorrow," she said with a smile.

So it worked, at least in some part!

For the moment, Durga was happy.

"It worked, guys!" Durga was smiling broadly. They were lounging in the garden after an early, elaborate breakfast with an Indian selection of idli, dosa, vada, upma, plus bread toast, butter, a selection of jams, fruit salad in fresh cream, teamed with a choice of freshly squeezed juices. Various pastries, frosted eclairs, and a large chocolate fudge cake made up the dessert.

Janice, Keith, and Abhik were relieved to see their buddy smiling again.

"So tell us everything," asked Keith.

"On an impulse, I slipped the Kshirakakoli herb in their orange juice, and by morning, they were up. That means these herbs might have helped in quickening the healing process!"

They all nodded.

"But curiously, my father's memory has not come back. My mother has recovered somewhat," added Durga looking slightly depressed.

"Well, it's just two days, Durga. Rest and care should help him get back to normal," assured Abhik.

Durga felt better.

Chapter Five

A Disaster and An Opportunity

Durga's parents were back home from the hospital. For now, elaborate arrangements were made for their stay at the Devdi. On her grandmother's suggestion, Durga and her friends returned to school.

The minute they got back to school, there was plenty to do: unattended homework, preparation for the essay, and the Cultural Secretary campaign.

Durga welcomed the rigorous schedule as it kept her from thinking about her parents.

The campaigning for Cultural Secretary became progressively messier as Durga, Janice, Abhik, and Keith plodded to keep things in balance. Racked by events going haywire, loud denouncements, and endless unreasonable requests, all masterfully orchestrated by Akanksha and her team, Durga and the team were irritated and exhausted. Durga knew who was behind all this but decided to do nothing about it..

Desperate for a break, Durga wandered into the library to borrow new books. She directly went to the mystery books section and picked up a few. As she passed the corridor, her eyes involuntarily rested on a large scroll painting hanging near the entrance. It was a Pattachitra.

Suddenly, she realized she had forgotten entirely about the parchment scroll in her sword! She walked to her secret corner in the library and opened the image she had clicked on her phone. She decided to do some homework on Soma, the herb mentioned in the parchment. There were so many academic resources on it.

Soma was believed to have the medicinal power to keep the human body from degeneration.

Why was the sloka on the left of the parchment talking about poison, then?

Idly, she browsed through some of the books in the reference section. Her eyes caught the title — *The Book of Poisons in India* — by Dr. Kennedy Chandrasekhar, Janice's father.

She picked it up and flipped through some pages. The book outlined poisons as silent weapons capable of destroying life mysteriously, secretly, and without violence.

A verse in Sanskrit read.

'Jalam visravayet sarmavamavisravyam ca dusayet,'

Which was translated as: *Waters of wells were to be mixed with poison and thus polluted* — This quote was attributed to Chanakya.

She felt exhausted and walked up to Librarian Swati Bhoopal, an erudite, well-informed, yet friendly lady, to check-in the books she had borrowed. Durga felt comfortable with her, and they often got into long conversations.

"Ha! Nice combination here. May I suggest another one?" asked Swati Bhoopal, looking over her reading glasses and handing over a biography of Janaki Ammal.

Durga nodded politely.

"You know, it wouldn't have been easy for her. She was India's first female botanist who helped identify and conserve the biodiversity of India. She led a tough life," Swati Bhoopal paused solemnly.

"I heard about how you saved Shiva. None of us would have even guessed that it was because of those flowers…it comes to you naturally…"

Durga looked up.

"Our ancient generations knew how important plants were, for the very survival of this planet. But now, we are destroying them mindlessly in the name of civilization. Natural Historian David Attenborough says only 40% of green cover is left on the Earth. We need another dynamic young lady like Janaki Ammal who can help bring back the love for plants in these times."

Swati Bhoopal looked at the books. Picking up the book on poisons, she said, "This, you can borrow only for one day.

It is from the restricted section."

She added the warning, "Be very careful!" Durga nodded and turned back towards her room, carrying the books.

Back in her hostel room, Durga kept the books on the table and decided to go for a walk. When she came back, *The Book of Poisons in India* was gone! Shocked, she called Janice, who said she had never returned to the room. A deflated Durga decided to attend her music class and come back to tackle this problem. The book was sitting on the table when she returned to the room. An icy chill settled on her heart. Someone had been in their room!

Anxiously, she rummaged in her swimwear bag to check if the bunch of copper plates and her father's journal were there. And they were. *Thank God!*

At her wit's end, she slumped on the bed, and before she realised, sleep overcame her. Darkness fell, and a loud thump on the door woke her up. It was Janice who had come back from her dance class.

"Hey D, guess what happened? You know the new girl Sampreeti...she's so funny. Wait, are you okay?"

"Jen, can you please stop your jibber-jabber? I want to return to Bamma tomorrow and check on Amma and Nanna."

Janice glared.

"Now??? You want to go now? Just when I thought we were making progress. You can see how hard we are working to make this work. Look, Diggy, I understand you are worried about your parents, but I think being here with us will keep you busy rather than alone. By the way, it's time you stop being sorry for yourself and think about others too!"

Janice's straightforward manner stung Durga.

"Well, it's my parents who are not well. Not your's. And certainly not my idea to become the Head Girl. Why would it matter to you? You guys are all selfish. You are making me the poster girl for projecting yourselves. I don't NEED to do this!" screamed Durga angrily.

"Oh yes, Ms. Nose-up-in-the-air princess, finding excuses to run away. At every available opportunity! I mean, c'mon, if you are so caring, why can't you be straight for once? Why did you lose that quiz on purpose?"

"I didn't; I just couldn't remember!"

"I can't believe it. Knowing how easy that question was! On the other hand, you figured out the flowers that poisoned the garden boy and even th-that herb that saved your mother and father! Now, how did you do that?" demanded Janice.

"Well, maybe they are all freakish aberrations! you know, Maybe I have a dual personality!"

Both of them glared at each other.

Janice looked disappointed.

"Well, my passions are bubbling near the surface, I am not gonna lie, you know. And for the record, I am worried about your parents too. They ARE half mine, too! And they ARE getting better. We need to give them some time. Just by being worried, no problem can be solved."

For a few moments, both of them sulked.

"Well, we have bigger fish to fry...do you know someone's been to our room?" said Durga.

"Wh-what???" Janice was taken aback.

"Yes, the book, Uncle Kenny wrote. That one. I borrowed it from the library, and it went missing. Then suddenly, it appeared back on the table."

Janice stared. Durga paced up and down the room.

Durga's cell phone rang. She glanced at it and saw that it was Abhik.

"I wanted to tell you both something important. Can you both come out and meet us?" Abhik seemed rushed.

"Yes, of course, right away!"

Durga and Janice glanced at each other and raced out.

Abhik and Keith were waiting near their favorite spot.

"D, as I was getting to the cafeteria, I saw Charan Tej sneaking into your room, and then in about 10 minutes, he snuck out," said Abhik.

"Charan? Oh, he's a nice boy. Why would he do

something like that?" exclaimed Durga and Janice. Charan's father was an auto driver, and his mother was a maid at somebody's home. Charan was an exceptionally bright student and was admitted to school just because of his talent. For Akanksha, this was unacceptable since Charan belonged to the Dalit community. And she was bent upon getting him into trouble.

"There must be a good reason. Unfortunately, he's caught on camera probably, and he will be expelled."

"We need to do something," said Durga anxiously.

It was getting late, but they had to act quickly.

"Well, let me make some calls to check how he got into this mess first," said Janice as she made some quick calls.

"Okay, my sources have found out that it was Ms. Burning Sensation at work," Janice sniffled angrily.

"Burning? Oh, I see...Akanksha! The name suits her," grinned Durga.

Just then, Charan Tej walked up to them. Janice was about to shout at him when Durga touched her friend's arm.

"I am sorry Durga Akka. I made a mistake. Akanksha Akka made me do it," Charan Tej volunteered on his own with tears in his eyes.

"It's okay, Charan. We will try to solve the problem," said Durga kindly. Visibly relieved, Charan walked away.

“Abhi, you are the IT wizard. Can anything be done? Like hacking into the security database and deleting the recording?” asked Janice.

“Well, no. Our school security systems are very outdated and manually operated. So I cannot log into them at all!” said Abhik.

They all sat thinking.

“Guys, we need to act quickly. The best thing would be to get hold of the camera recording. If we could erase the recording before tomorrow morning, there would be no proof,” said Keith. Everyone agreed.

“Okay. The only way is to get to the Security Office, where they keep the recordings. We need to sneak in somehow and erase the content. Let’s get some powerful torchlights, wear dark clothes, and meet near the Security office by midnight,” Janice suggested.

As per the plan, they met at midnight. Abhik and Keith hid behind a large tree facing the Security Office, keeping a watch. Durga and Janice perched behind a large mulberry bush near the entrance. “Hmm, these mulberries are good,” said Janice, nibbling on some ripe fruits hanging from the bush. Durga shushed her. Janice went quiet but did not stop nibbling. Durga sighed.

An hour later, they saw the security guards walking out for a smoke, leaving the room empty. Durga and Janice crept in, checked the feed, and erased the recording. They started back carefully, avoiding the spotlights that lit the extensive grounds.

A sudden movement ahead of them made them almost scream. They shrank further into the shadows, staring at the dark outlines of two people grappling. A torch flared.

"How dare you? Who are you? Is anyone around?" Akanksha was shouting.

Immediately, the school grounds were flooded with light.

"What's going on here? Akanksha, Jagannath, and Elizabeth, what are you three doing here at night? I am utterly disappointed. Thank god, Security Narsimha saw you sneaking out of your rooms at 11:00 and alerted me..." Professor Jaywant was shouting. She taught them Physics.

"You don't understand, Professor; there were two men here. Moreover, Durga and her friends are here. We saw them," whimpered Akanksha.

"What utter rubbish! How dare you tell such lies! I shall speak to your House Master. Wandering about at midnight! All of you will receive detention."

After they left, there was silence once again. Keith, Durga, Abhik, and Janice crept forward.

A few moments passed. Something brushed against Keith's arm lightly. There was a sharp cry and a scuffle in the ensuing confusion; Janice switched on both torches at once.

In the light, they could see it was Narasimha, their Head of Security.

Things couldn't get any worse after that!

Narasimha marched them down to Professor Jaywant's study on the first floor; excuses, alibis, raced around Durga's brain, each so incredulous that even she wouldn't believe them herself, let alone a teacher. At any rate, they couldn't reveal Akanksha's wicked plot.

Professor Jaywant appeared once again, looking crimson with anger.

"I would never have believed it of any of you. Narasimha says you were sneaking around the school grounds. It's midnight! Please explain what's going on here?" she asked furiously.

Contrite, they all stared fixedly at their feet.

"Oh, I think I've got a good idea of what's been going on," said Professor Jaywant. "It doesn't take a genius to work it out. You fed Akanksha and her friends some cock-and-bull story and made them come here so they would get into trouble. I've already caught them. I suppose you think it's funny?"

Except for Keith, who looked stunned and hurt, no one said anything.

"I'm disgusted," roared Professor Jaywant. "Seven students out of bed in one night! I've never heard of such a thing before! Durga, Abhik? I thought APJ Abdul Kalam House meant more to you than this. All of you will receive detentions. Now, please get back to your rooms."

Morning came. Durga received a summons to see Principal Roy. Her heart lurched.

Durga walked alone towards Principal Roy's room. As she entered the formidable room, Principal Roy signaled her to take a seat.

"Last night, our security camera feed also showed two men fleeing the grounds, proving that Akanksha Raju was indeed telling the truth. These two, although dressed in our staff uniform, aren't ours. What were they doing there, and how did they access our very secure systems?" said Principal Roy, sounding worried.

Durga looked up apprehensively.

"I strongly suggest that you don't take unnecessary risks. Is there anything you would like to tell me?" asked Principal Roy. Durga avoided her piercing gaze and hung her head.

"Nothing, Ma'am," she murmured.

"Don't worry about Charan Tej; we will not expel him. Next time, I suggest you talk to me before you decide to take things into your hands. You can go now."

Durga gulped.

"Yes, Ma'am. Thank you, Ma'am," muttered an

astonished Durga. Her respect for her Principal grew even more. *Nothing escaped her attention!*

As she walked back, her thoughts returned to the men.

Who were those men? And why were they sneaking around the school?

Instinctively, she returned to the spot where Akanksha and her friends had been caught the previous night. She wasn't sure what she was looking for. Just then, she caught sight of a small envelope covered with soil. She picked it up. Inside was a small sapling. And a note with four words: *Find Adrian Gerber, Germany.*

Chapter Six

A New Discovery

"What is the scientific name of this plant?"

Professor Lata Anantanarayan's voice, heavily laced with a distinct Tamil accent, boomed across the room. She was the Head of Life Sciences and taught Botany with an inexhaustible passion. She was thin, wiry, rather bird-like, and upright. Dressed in a traditional Kanjeevaram saree, her hair tied into a tight chignon, she had the habit of staring unblinkingly at her students through large oversized thick spectacles that perched on her beaky nose. And they stared back.

Professor Anantanarayan shrugged impatiently and summed up the class once again. *Bright but lazy*. Holding the plant aloft like it was some beacon, she strode purposefully across the room towards the back benches. A soft murmur went around the room. But no one dared to answer the question. Professor Anantanarayan, was precisely the sort of woman who intensely disapproved of guessing instead of 'knowing' the correct answer.

"Janice, why so quiet today?"

Janice stood up and looked around the class smugly.

"Alternanthera sessilis. It is an aquatic plant, and its leaves are used as a vegetable."

"Excellent, Janice!" muttered Professor Anantanarayan approvingly, nearly crushing the plant in her efficient fists before returning to her desk.

Janice beamed, lapping up some more of the admiring glances before settling down.

Durga rolled her eyes disdainfully.

"Why are we doing this activity? Identifying plants?" demanded Professor Anantanarayan. Silence reigned. She looked around petulantly and continued.

"Let me give you a broad perspective. India has one of the most varied germplasm, which means that we have several different species of flora and fauna here. They hold the key to all breeding activities — in simpler terms, to come out with plant varieties that have an ideal combination of characteristics such as improved crop yield, better disease, and pest resistance. Now, can one of you tell me one more reason why India needs to conserve its germplasm?"

Abhik's hand went up.

"Yes?"

"India has a unique history of traditional medicine. Knowing our plant resources can help us develop ways to integrate traditional medicinal plants into modern healthcare solutions. Countries like Thailand, for instance, are trying this out."

"Very good, Abhik! Thank you! What we need to do more seriously, is to systematically study how many plant species are there, classify them and then create some means of conserving them for the future. It's still a task in progress. All of you can contribute towards this cause," Professor Anantanarayan said passionately.

"Let's get back to the exercise. Identify this plant for me, please?" Professor Anantanarayan's shrilly voice rose to another alarming level.

"Orange Jessamine or Murraya paniculate from the family of Jasmine. Not of Indian origin. It has medicinal properties as well," drawled Elizabeth.

"Very good, Elizabeth! But I do ardently wish..." Professor Anantanarayan stopped mid-sentence, glanced pointedly at Durga, and quipped, "…some more of you would be interested in participating in my class as well. That would be a great change."

Durga shrugged nervously. Answering in class was a nightmare of the worst kind for her. *Words get stuck in my throat*. Thankfully, the bell rang, and the class came to an end. Without looking back, Professor Anantanarayan left. The class got noisy again.

“Don’t let all the attention get to your pretty heads, Hoity Toities,” the sniggering voice of Akanksha made Durga and Janice turn around. Abhik was wheeling out of the classroom and collecting Nibble’s cage while Keith was gathering their backpacks.

“On the contrary. You seem to be longing for some. What’s with you now??” demanded Janice.

“Me? Look, dear Ms. Menace, I am here to give some serious advice. Especially to you, Durga. I am asking you to withdraw your senseless nomination for the post of Cultural Secretary. You are out of your Lagaan league here. You have no personality. Nobody even notices you. So, stop wasting everybody’s time and go back to your beloved library. That’s where you belong.”

Durga stood silently, feeling deflated.

Janice flew into a rage. Abhik and Keith came around to be next to them.

“Go back and replan your battle moves. We are here to fight,” Abhik said in a quiet and challenging manner. Many students gathered around them.

A spellbound Durga turned to look at Abhik, who seldom spoke, let alone argued.

Go where you’re lookin’; look where you’re goin’ growled Nibbles in his best Clint Eastwood imitation.

A moment’s stunned silence later, Akanksha glared at

Nibbles, shrugged dramatically, and strode out of the classroom, followed by Jagannath and Elizabeth.

In the afternoon, Durga texted *Library* to her friends. Within minutes, Janice, Keith, and Abhik joined her in their usual place in the library.

"Look at this," said Durga, showing the envelope with the sapling.

"What? Where did you find this?" wondered Keith, taking the envelope from Durga's hands and examining it.

Quietly, Durga took out her magnifying glass and scrutinized the sapling.

"I found this envelope with the sapling on the grounds where we had a scuffle with those intruders last night. This plant is rare, and it's Begonia Tessaricarpa. Look at the plant's flowers with four distinct petals — two large and two small ones. My father had unearthed this plant during his trip to Arunachal Pradesh in Northeastern India."

Abhik, Janice, and Keith watched Durga curiously. They had not seen this side of her. She seemed to brim with confidence. *She is so brilliant! How could she lose that quiz?* wondered Keith silently as he watched her, fascinated.

"This plant is supposed to be extinct and rediscovered by my father after 115 years. It is called Buckuchurbu by the local tribals," described Durga in a matter-of-fact voice.

There was a stunned silence. For a moment, nobody said anything. Keith was the first to recover.

"Durga, are you sure?" he asked.

"I am 100% sure, Keith. I was a part of that expedition. You will find the details about this plant in the Red Book, which mentions endangered plants in immediate need of conservation. My father's paper on it is also available in the online resources."

Abhik checked online resources immediately and found that Durga was completely accurate.

"She's 100% right," confirmed Abhik.

"Wow, D, you ARE the chhupa-one, very very chhupa!" exclaimed Keith.

Durga went red.

"How is this important? I mean, the plant?" asked Janice, entirely at sea.

"It's an extremely rare medicinal plant. Tribal people use the plant to treat severe stomach-related ailments. This envelope with the sapling might have been with Dr. Uwe. Maybe that's why those men were on our school grounds the next day. Hard to guess at this point. They were probably searching for this when we appeared on the scene…"

"Why was he killed then?" wondered Janice.

"Look, Jenny. Reports suggest that he may have died of

Aconitum poisoning, as Durga initially suggested. His death may have been accidental…" said Abhik.

"Somehow…"

"Stop, Jenny. Let's not get distracted at this point. Keith and Abhik — Google this Adrian Gerber, and find out as much as possible. Janice and I will find out where this plant sample came from."

"Yes, boss," smiled Abhik and Keith, marveling at Durga's decisive manner.

Durga and Janice started walking. "What's the plan?" asked Janice.

"Let's ask Professor Lata Anantanarayan if she can accompany us to the Department of Biodiversity. Dr. Pinnasetty, my father's old colleague, might tell us if this plant sample was in a lab or something," said Durga thoughtfully.

Janice messaged their teacher immediately. "Diggy, Professor Anantanarayan will meet us at the Teachers' Lounge in five."

As they neared the Lounge, Professor Anantanrayan turned around and motioned them to sit.

"Ma'am we wanted to ask if we could visit the Department of Biodiversity. My father's old friend, Dr. Pinnasetty, is the Head of the Department there. We wanted to a few resources from there for our preparation for the upcoming Quiz competition in Germany," requested Durga.

Professor Lata Anantanarayan beamed.

"Well, you are in luck. I was planning to visit Dr. Pinnasetty this afternoon. Both of you can come with me. Be at the Grand Porch in 15 minutes."

"Thank you, Ma'am."

Durga and Janice set out to the Grand Porch. The sun had come out brilliantly, and the Cassia Fistula trees in the campus presented a charming sight with their cascading yellow summer blooms.

The Grand Porch was quite distinguished. Spacious and rectangular, made entirely with rough-cut red bricks and wooden flooring, it housed a large reception desk, a magazine rack, and mismatched furniture that lent the place an air of chic. Next to the entrance was a lush magnolia tree with pale pink blossoms.

Both strolled up and greeted the chirpy receptionist Mala Mani, who habitually dressed up 'like a Christmas tree,' as Janice would scornfully say. In precisely 15 minutes, a white Innova drew up. Durga and Janice jogged towards it and got in.

They reached the Department in 20 minutes and were ushered straight into one of the labs.

The botanical lab was roomy and with old-fashioned furniture. A rectangular table stood in the center of the room, on which stood several glass flasks, each with a small plant suspended in the middle. The table was surrounded by a team of botanists in lab coats peering at them and taking notes. They all looked up as Durga and Janice entered the room along with Professor Anantanarayan.

Several came forward and eagerly shook hands with Durga.

Durga felt an automatic pleasure as she heard glowing tributes being paid to her father.

"Hello, Professor Anantanarayan; I am glad you are all here," said a large, thick-set man with hardly any neck in a voluminous white coat. He was Dr. Bhagirath Pinnasetty, Head of the Division of Biodiversity.

"You may not know me, but I greatly admire your father's work, Durga. I am sorry about the news about your parents. But I heard they are getting better. Yes? These things take time, na? Meanwhile, I am glad to see you and Janice here. How is your father, Dr. Chandrasekhar? I heard he's in Cambridge lecturing. Yes? Oh, good. Please convey my regards to him, Janice. Now, how can I help you, Madam?" asked Dr. Pinnasetty, as they settled in their chairs.

"Thank you, Dr. Pinnasetty. I request you to give a guest lecture at our school at a convenient date," said Professor Lata Anantanarayan

"It would be my privilege, madam. I will let you know the dates."

"Thank you, Dr. Pinnasetty. Now, Durga and Janice had some doubts and needed some help."

Durga spoke up. "Sir, I wanted some information on Begonia Tessaricarpa. My father mentioned that a few samples were sent here after his expedition. I would like to see one. Does it grow in these parts?"

"Why, of course. There was one sample here. Yes, your father had discovered it. And to answer your question, no. The plant does not grow here. The samples are from Arunachal Pradesh."

"Can we see it?" Durga persisted.

"Yes, come," Dr. Pinnasetty got up and took them towards one of the jars.

Janice, Durga, and Professor Anantanarayan stood beside him.

"This is the one. We have sent the other samples to the Centre of Biodiversity, New Delhi, for analysis. Why don't you come back after a few months, Durga? I can show more samples of the same," said Dr. Pinasetty, with a smile.

"Thank you, sir. I will do that. Can we borrow the book -— *The Flora of the Udaipur Wildlife Sanctuary, West Champaran* on your table?" asked Durga.

"Sure! Here it is. You are very observant, Durga. You can return it whenever you are done with it," said Dr. Pinnasetty genially.

"Thank you, Dr. Pinnasetty. We will take leave now," said Professor Anantanarayan, getting up. Dr. Pinnasetty ushered them out.

The three of them were silent as they reached the school. Durga and Janice strolled back to their rooms.

"Well, there goes the clue. If the plant doesn't grow here, what was it doing in the cover?"

Durga stopped and looked at Janice.

"Dr. Pinnasetty was lying. The plant he showed was NOT Begonia Tessaricarpa. Although, it did look the same. I hope you noticed how he went white when I asked him about it, Jenny. Also, I noticed a watch on the table. It was a very unusual one, and could have belonged to Dr. Uwe Schmitt. That's why I asked to borrow that book."

Janice stared.

"H-how in the world..?"

"Remember the day I walked over to check those flowers? I happened to see the dead man quite closely. He was wearing a Micky Mouse watch, a funny thing for an adult. Don't you think?"

"Yes," gasped Janice.

"Well, I am now certain of two things. Dr. Pinnasetty is somehow connected to the death of that man and plant theft. Those men at our school were definitely searching for the envelope with the plant specimen of Begonia Tessaricarpa," said Durga thoughtfully.

"That is a stupendous deduction, Diggy! Marvelous!!" exclaimed Janice.

Durga shrugged.

"Well, let's ask if our guys found anything on Adrian Gerber."

A dollop of the early morning sun had lit up everything around them. The leaves and flowers seemed to be sparkling. The air was fresh. A lone cuckoo was singing melodiously.

Abhik sat frowning over his laptop. Keith was sipping his 'sparkling water,' a German habit he found hard to let go of. Janice was biting away at a piece of toast. The cafeteria was very quiet at this time of the morning.

"Hmm… Adrian is quite an interesting guy. It turns out he's a child prodigy— an only child of his rather impoverished parents of mixed lineage. At 20, he received double Doctorates from the University of Berlin, Germany, and Cambridge in Plant Genetics and Entomology. Adrian has a company called "Seltenheit GmbH" that 'sources' rare plants for 'enthusiastic gardeners'. Here is his picture," reeled off Abhik.

"Now, thaaat is certainly a coincidence!" said Durga, quietly looking at the picture of Adrian.

"Yes, Diggy, na?"

"I agree," said Abhik.

"Aren't we going to Cologne this year for that quiz?" murmured Durga thoughtfully.

"Diggy, but let's not jump to any conclusions. It could be just a coincidence?" said Keith.

"Okay. Let's regroup after lunch. It's time for some cookies and campaign plans," said Janice. Everyone nodded.

Only Durga wrinkled her nose. No one paid much attention to that!

Chapter Seven

Too Many Letdown Moments

"THIS is not going well," Janice's face was crimson red. She tried to call Durga on her cell phone. Radio silence greeted her. Keith and Abhik looked up at the empty altar again as if some miracle would make their friend appear. Durga had gone missing again. The hopeful crowd gathered around, holding small placards printed with the *Vote for D* sign, shuffled restlessly.

Slowly, the crowd moved towards Akanksha, who was dressed like a Pinterest model and was hollering away into the microphone in her sing-song voice.

"FRIENDS, WHERE IS MY OPPONENT? WHAT CAN SHE DO WHEN SHE CANNOT FIND TIME EVEN TO BE HERE?" she bellowed.

"This will give a great opportunity for Akku," murmured Keith. Abhik sighed and looked away.

Janice and Keith plopped on a few empty chairs.

"Wonder where she could be?" murmured Janice, looking stricken.

Night had fallen and yet there was no sign of Durga.

"Are we all putting too much pressure on her?" wondered Keith before they all went back to their rooms.

Janice disagreed. However, a small doubt kept nagging her. On Janice's insistence, Durga had, in fact, made many changes after coming back from holidays. From her dressing to practising her speeches, of course, pretty reluctantly. Janice had been overjoyed to see her doing these and constantly boasted to Abhik and Keith about how Durga was making 'great strides.' Abhik, on his part, researched and came up with clever ideas for publicity material, and Keith went all out in creating groups to support Durga in her campaign.

Though there were still a couple of months left before the actual election date, Akanksha had upped the game by starting her act early. This made Durga's team kickstart their campaign to match their opponent's pace.

Unknown to her friends, Durga simmered inside while keeping an outward calm. She didn't want to disappoint them. She dreaded the day of the speech-making. Finally, Durga balked.

I cannot, she whispered to herself and hid alone in the library until it was time to leave. *I am a geeky, quiet person focused on becoming a space scientist. I am NOT suitable for leadership roles.*

A horrible sense of guilt enveloped her. *I have let down my friends.* Feeling miserable, she collected her books and started walking back alone from the library towards her room, determined to announce her decision to her friends.

The pathway was lonely.

I shouldn't have stayed back for so long! Durga thought nervously.

Just ahead, she heard muffled voices. They seemed to be arguing. Frantically, she checked out if there were any security guards around. There were none. Instinctively, she hid behind a bush, her heart thumping.

"I didn't find the envelope nor the journal in the girl's room. I searched the whole place!"

"Hmm, maybe the information we got about the envelope on Dr. Uwe was wrong. About the journal, KM most certainly said he saw her putting it in her backpack. Maybe he was mistaken! Still, it was worth a try. At least KM got the mobile phone of Dr. Uwe from the other girls room. That might give us some clues," said another gruff voice.

A few moments of silence ensued.

"Dr. Harish will get back his memory any day now. We need to get our act together soon. We need to figure out a way to…"

A horrified Durga heard a muffled shriek followed by a heavy thump. She closed her mouth with both hands to keep from crying out.

"Who is this guy? I think he was following us and listening in! Anyway, this one will be quiet for some time. Let's get out of here," commanded the other voice.

After some scraping noises, a thump, and a grunt, there was silence again. The men seemed to have left.

Durga sat frozen.

What happened here? Why are these men talking about her father and the journal? Panic gripped her, and she felt inside her bag. The journal and the copper plates were right there!

For several moments, Durga didn't dare to stir. Finally, she gathered her courage and stepped out of the bush. There seemed to be no one.

However, to her intense horror, she saw a body lying across the path. Durga ran to the spot.

The man with a greyish beard, and a simple white kurta-pyjama had an ugly gash on his head. He was turned to the side and seemed to be bleeding. His eyes were closed, and his breathing, laborious.

Durga fumbled in her pocket for her mobile. Just as she was about to dial, she felt a firm grip on her hand. Durga shrieked. The man sat up and fixed her with his steely gaze. To Durga's intense surprise, the man seemed friendly and calm. His eyes seemed to light up looking at her.

"I am so lucky to have found you. Listen to me carefully, Your Highness. Keep your father's journal and the copper plates extremely safe. They will lead you to your quest.

Yattadagre vishameva parinaamemritopapam tatsukham saattvikam proktamaatmabuddhiprasaadajam

"You are now the custodian. To save the world. Take care of yourself! I am a well-wisher. Goodbye!" The man got up quickly, pulled a handkerchief from his pocket, held it up to his wound, and disappeared into the darkness.

Panic gripped her as she ran back to her room. The minute she entered, Janice sprang upon her like an angry kitten, "Where were you? You know how disappointed we all are, D?"

Durga felt faint. She buckled and fell into the arms of Janice, who caught her in time and laid her on the couch.

Janice felt a wave of extreme remorse. *Diggy is sensitive. Poor thing. Have I forced her into too much?*

Janice ordered some juice from the cafeteria.

It was nearly an hour by the time Durga woke up.

Her head felt a bit light, but she sat up, staring at the anxious face of her friend.

"I am sorry. I let you down," Durga managed to murmur.

"We are sorry to have pushed you, Diggy," said Janice.

Janice went and sat next to Durga and held her hand.

"Jenny, I need to tell you something."

Durga told Janice about the voices she heard and the wounded man.

Janice sat stunned.

"Shall we go to the spot and check, Jenny?"

They both ran back to the spot. There was no evidence of anyone being there!

"Should we inform the security, D?"

"What good would that do, Jenny? The man is long gone. What did he mean by my quest? What is my quest? How can he know so much about Nanna and me? I also forgot to tell you guys that my sword has a secret parchment, and that man recited the sloka from it!"

"What sloka? Which parchment? What are you talking about?"

"Let's call the others."

In a few moments, they all gathered in the Common Hall. Durga narrated her entire ordeal and also about the secret parchment.

They took turns looking at the parchment.

Abhik scanned it and ran a search in his database. Nothing came up except the sloka from the Bhagavad Gita.

"Well, it's been an exhausting day. Let's call it a night. Maybe tomorrow will bring better ideas," said Keith, yawning. All of them agreed.

Durga crept into her bed. When sleep wouldn't come, she took out the journal, but did not find anything outstanding. Finally, she yawned, shut the book, and fell asleep.

"Diggy, wake up. WAKE UP," Janice's exasperated voice woke up Durga.

"What, Jenny? Stop screaming. What happened?" asked Durga groggily.

"Well, the mean Akku has published a podcast on you in the Blast On."

Blast On was the school's unofficial gossip-mongering podcast, which broadcasted all sorts of sensational goings-on around the campus.

Before Durga could stop her, Janice played the podcast.

Where is D? Where is D-ee? Disappeared into thin air, oi?

Despite her trusted team's well-meaning best efforts at rustling up some lackluster placards and half-hearted group messages, there is NOTHING about D that we know.

What is she as a person? This leads us to the many rumors circulating about D. That she dislikes mingling with ordinary folks because of her Royal blah-blah background? That she has palaces where people have homes? That she looks down upon us because we are not as intellectual as her?

She hates crowds and chocolate! I mean, what sort of creatures can hate chocolate? Now, the most critical question. Why does she always run away? How can we elect her as our leader? On that reflective note, I am signing off..

Fury rose in Durga. She flung the blanket fiercely to the floor.

Janice laughed. Durga stood flabbergasted.

"What"

"Diggy, it's perfect. You will now be famous. And you have our sweet Akku to give credit to. People will now notice and observe you! They will now look up to you. You are a royal, the silent type; you are serious..."

Durga put her hands to her head. "But that's exactly what I don't want. I don't want people looking at me. Moreover, I messed up yesterday. I don't want to..."

"Oh, that! Don't you worry. It was just ONE meeting. You might have had an emergency of some sort. We will handle that one," said Janice lightly.

Durga groaned.

Janice gave her some cold water and a banana.

"Bananas contain a natural chemical which can make people feel happy. Right?"

Durga laughed.

"Let's get going, Diggy. Our class starts in 5 minutes,"

Durga anxiously checked her messages. There was one from Bamma. Her parents were fine! Heaving a sigh of relief, she video-called her mom.

"Amma, I miss you. How are things over there?" asked Durga.

"Things are better. How's it there?" asked her mother.

"Everything is okay," smiled Durga.

"I am glad about that! I want you to be strong and focus on school for a bit. Don't worry about Dad; he's a strong man. He will recover soon."

Durga nodded thoughtfully.

They made their way to their classes. At lunchtime, they received a message from Professor Jaywant to meet her in the labs in the evening. *She's not forgotten detention.* Durga thought, wondering how bad it would be.

As they neared the Physics lab, the setting sun created an orange hue around the globe sculpted into an engraved Aryabatta statuette on the top of the building. Durga pushed open a large oak door roughly hewn with bronzed metallic girdles. A blast of cool air brushed their faces as they entered the corridor. The traditional limestone and clay building was naturally cool and ambient, with light streaming through the large windows on either side. Principal Roy's vision was instrumental in the school's unusual design and architecture.

They entered the now-empty lab with several large desks and conceptual demo equipment. Professor Jaywant sat hunched in her comfortably stuffed chair that overlooked the garden, dressed in worn-out jeans and a T-shirt. They could hear the bustle of Akanksha, Elizabeth, and Jagannath coming through as they lined up in the lab.

Professor Jaywant looked at both of the groups and motioned them to sit. Clearing her throat, she said, “Instead of the usual detention, here’s something you all will take up. Akanksha, Elizabeth, and Jagannath, you three will teach lessons to street children at Rainbow Orphanage, within walking distance from here, for one month, and conduct a workshop with them on a topic of your choice. Please meet Mr. Narasimha at the gate tomorrow, and he will accompany you. You three may go now.”

Scowling deeply, Akanksha, Elizabeth, and Jagannath turned and walked away in a huff, muttering indiscreetly, “How disappointing — we could do better stuff.”

Turning to Durga, Jaywant said, “You and your friends here have to do two activities. First, go to the Maithree Old Age Home for one month and help around. Second, take up the ‘Clean the Beach’ activity for the forthcoming month. You will get two days a week for these beginning tomorrow. Our security personnel will accompany you. Note that you will not receive any leniency whatsoever regarding your academics. You will have to keep up with it too.”

“What made you romp the grounds at that time of the night anyway? Don’t you know how unsafe it is?”

No one said anything and looked steadily at their feet.

"All right, off you go."

"Awesome! That wasn't bad," exclaimed Keith

"It certainly is a noble activity," whispered Abhik.

Durga, Janice, Keith, and Abhik reported to the Maithree Old Age home the next day.

The home was surprisingly large, with extensive gardens and fruit trees. Many elders were either walking or being wheeled in chairs across the pathway. Some of them sat under a large banyan tree, reading a newspaper. They all looked up curiously at Durga and her friends. The first thing they noticed was how ill-kept the place was. Peeling paint on moist-looking walls, old plastic chairs, harried staff in worn-out uniforms trudging across, tea served in thin plastic disposable glasses, a snoring security guard, the list went on. Abhik was particularly upset that there was only one ramp with broken tiles.

They were ushered hurriedly into the Chief Administrator's Office by one of the 'peons' who wore a funny hat and no uniform. The room was filled with knick-knacks of various kinds, and a dusty shelf with many mementos, now faded. Durga noticed a large picture of her Grandfather, Rajasaheb, covered with dust and thick cobwebs.

In the center of the room was a large wooden desk piled with old-fashioned files and plastic baskets filled with papers. Occupying a high wooden chair was a vigorous sixty-odd woman with iron-grey hair, a determined chin and an indifferent expression. It was Mrs. Mallika Roberts.

Durga, Janice, Keith, and Abhik gathered at the side of her table. Mrs. Roberts cleared her throat, looked at Durga, and gave something suspiciously like a nod. Mrs. Roberts did not even acknowledge the others and started speaking, looking at no one.

"So you are here to spend some time as some punishment for all the wicked things you did in school? Wonder why they send me only spoilt kids... Well, I suppose they want you all to learn from me and my example. I was a super good student and won many awards and no wonder I am head of this prestigious institution, while you are sure to become no-gooders. Even you, Princess? I can't believe the arrogance! Well, all that money is sure to go to your head. No wonder you get detentions! Remember, crowns don't make princesses," she added disparagingly while Durga looked down apologetically.

Janice, Keith, and Abhik went crimson with anger.

"Well, you all have nothing to do, and I HAVE to work to keep this institution running daily without funds or any encouragement from anyone. Anyway, from tomorrow, I am going away on personal work for a month. I have put Ms. Jeena in charge. So go, and enjoy your time. You can browse and watch movies for all I care. You can go."

Having said this, brimming with wrath, Mrs. Roberts turned away and started working on her laptop. Durga, Janice, Keith, and Abhik were hustled away by the 'peon' from the room and made to sit outside on a long porch.

"What just happened in there? Diggy, you can't take this lying down. She insulted you, and you said nothing? For how many years will you be a coward, Diggy? I am fed up, fed up," jumped Janice angrily. Keith tried to calm Janice.

Durga burst into tears. Abhik wheeled himself close to her. "It's not easy being who you are, D. You must try harder."

Janice rushed to Durga's side. "Diggy, it is for your own good. You have it in you, hiding somewhere. Get it out!" said Janice more gently.

Just then, a rather sad-looking, rake-thin lady in a threadbare nurse's uniform rushed towards them.

"Hello, I am Jeena. Er, welcome to our home for the aged. Even though it is not much," she glanced unhappily around and continued, "we try to keep our inmates fed at least once daily. They have no choice; they have nowhere to go."

Durga, Janice, Keith, and Abhik turned to look at Jeena, who was going all jibber-jabber without a pause.

"Well, the plumbing is old, there is no money for medicine, no decent food, and these walls... moist and anyone can easily get sick. The bed linen haven't been replaced in over five years and are threadbare. And you rich kids from a fancy school would like to spend some time here just because you guys have been naughty. What can I say? You can do anything you like, and just keep me informed," paused Jeena, looking at them scornfully.

Durga, Janice, Keith, and Abhik said nothing. Finally, it was Durga who cleared her throat.

"Ms. Jeena, sit down for a minute. Will you?"

"Princess, you can call me Jeena."

"And you can drop the Princess. I am Durga, and my friends are Janice, Keith, and Abhik. Can you please show us around?"

Jeena nodded quickly and escorted them to the kitchen, a vast, unkempt backyard, and the library.

"Dirty, badly maintained, this place looks like a hell hole!" exclaimed Keith.

The rumble of a car driving off was heard.

"Well, there she goes, dumping this place on my head. How am I supposed to maintain this place?" plonked Jeena onto a rickety wooden stool.

"Jeena Akka, Jeena Akka, 405 Taatagaaru uncle has a stomachache," a young boy came running to the spot where they stood.

"Oh, poor thing, I have no medicine to give him," groaned Jeena.

"Jeena, can you take us there?" asked Durga

Jeena nodded, and they all went to room 405, where they saw an old man lying on a cot, holding his stomach and crying in pain.

Durga opened her laptop bag and drew out the herb powder.

"Jeena, I have some herb powder with me. Just ask someone to get me half a glass of milk."

Even before Jeena said anything, the boy rushed to the kitchen and brought a small glass of milk. Durga mixed some powder and gave it to the old man to drink. In about 15 minutes, he sat up, feeling better!

The old man kept making namaskarams to Durga, who waved it away, embarassed. Janice, Keith, and Abhik gave a fist bump to Durga. Jeena stood there with tears in her eyes.

"Oh, thank you, Princess! I mean D-Durga. You are a wonderful person. I wish we had someone like you to help us restore this place to its former glory! My father was the manager here. I grew up here. It was quite well maintained in those days. Then, he died, and I became an orphan. Mrs. Roberts came and took charge. I was grateful that she did not turn me out. You see, even I have no place to go!"

Durga listened quietly. Janice's mobile trilled. It was time to get back to school.

All of them bade goodbye to Jeena and got back to school.

Durga didn't say much all evening. Janice, Keith, and Abhik assumed she was upset about the argument in the afternoon.

Chapter Eight

Making the Most of Detention

"Guys, let's do something about this old age home," bluttered out Durga when they were all having breakfast.

"Sure, let's talk to Queen Mother and..."

"Jenny, no! It's our detention. Let's do it our way. Let's make it meaningful," said Durga firmly.

"Wow, nice idea. This is a good decision, D," said Keith admiringly. Abhik thumbs-upped.

"Okay, here's the plan D. First, let's go there and analyze how much the place needs in terms of expenditure. And then we can plan," said Abhik.

On Friday morning, they were back at the old age home.

Jeena showed them all the bills and the records hidden in Mrs. Robert's bureau.

"Ah, Mrs. Roberts is corrupt and has been diverting all the funding!" exclaimed Abhik and Keith, who had analyzed all the pretty apparent transactions.

Then, they made a tour of the entire facility, making notes about what parts of the building could be mended, what could be added, repaired, and restored.

"I read this wonderful article in a magazine. We can turn the backyard into a large kitchen garden, get some vegetable & fruit plants from the nurseries, add a brood of chicken for eggs, four black buffaloes for milk, and a borewell for water facilities," suggested Janice.

"I found out from my parents that we can plaster the places where the walls are moist and get them painted with waterproof material. Also, some of the beds can be repaired at a minimal cost. I spoke to a carpenter and a mason. They can do it in two weeks," said Keith.

"We can ask Arjuna Steels based in Hyderabad to contribute their social causes fund. The MD is my mother's patient. I can check on this," said Abhik

"Great. How much money do we need for all this, Jeena?" asked Durga.

"Well, about 10-12 lakhs, give a rupee or two. After we streamline all the funding, and cutting off Mrs. Robert's corrupt vendors," said Jeena, working on the financials.

Durga sighed. "Well, that's a lot! I think we would have to ask Bamma," murmured Durga dejectedly.

"Not necessary. I can raise it through crowdfunding!

There you go. I already created a link. Just send this out to various patrons, Jeena, and I will post it on my wall. I am sure we can raise at least some of the amount in no time," said Abhik

"Wow, that's great!" exclaimed Durga

"Okay, here you are! About nine lakhs have already been deposited in the last four days. That's the power of crowdfunding," said Abhik smugly

"And Arjuna Steels are giving us cots, blankets, cutlery, and chairs worth two lakh rupees," said Janice happily.

"Great, we can keep some amount aside for day-to-day running and use the rest. Let's get to work," said Durga.

Durga's mind was constantly on the parchment, but she could do nothing. There was simply no free time.

In three weeks, the old age home was looking very different. The backyard flourished with rows of luscious vegetable patches, a herb garden, hybrid fruit trees, and a chicken brood that became the source of eggs. Durga took every opportunity to test the recipes from the copper plates and her father's journal to come up with some quick, safe remedies to help the inmates. She was surprised at how familiar it all felt and remembered her father's words — *It comes to you naturally*. She wondered if this was actually true!

Janice single-handedly planned the dairy farm with five buffaloes and three cows supplying milk, cream, fresh butter, and ghee. Donations kept coming in, and the cutlery, bed linen, curtains were all changed. Keith oversaw the plumbing and painting. The common room was fitted with a large format TV. Additional ramps for wheelchairs were built. The garden was cleaned, and several park benches were installed under the banyan tree. Abhik continued to run a social campaign, posting updates every day to all the donors, which helped to bring in more donations. Not only did he get the Internet installed, but he also helped to download an app that streamlined all the institution's financial transactions. Jeena created a well-thought-out menu and a timetable for the inmates and staff.

"We are so thankful, Durgamma. The medicine you gave was so helpful. You have a gift. It comes to you from your father. So, will you become a botanist like him?" asked Captain Arun Sharma, one of the inmates. He didn't have any family. Durga found herself talking to him a lot.

"I don't know yet, Uncle Sharma. I want to become a space scientist, actually."

He looked at her and nodded.

"Hmm. Ok," he murmured.

"The medicine you gave was so bitter, Durgamma, but it worked wonders. You are our savior," mumbled a toothless old lady who shuffled towards them and held Durga's hands appreciatively. All the inmates had become like an extended family to them.

"*Yattadagre vishameva parinaamemritopapam,*

tatsukham saattvikam proktamaatmabuddhiprasaadajam,

says the Gita," quoted Captain Sharma.

Durga looked at him, stunned. But his serene smile calmed her. *Well, if those lines are from the Gita, anyone could know them.*

"What do the lines mean, Uncle?"

"It's philosophy. Shri Krishna said that the spiritual path is tough, but in the end, it is as pleasant as nectar. To find happiness, one must engage in activities that require discipline, sacrifice, or patience but lead to lasting peace and fulfilment. It's like taking medicine that tastes bitter. However, it results in true well-being in the long run. You are too young for all this. Yet, you are already providing us with Soma, the nectar," smiled Captain Sharma.

Once again, Durga was startled.

Soma. There is no time to think about that now! She shrugged.

For the first time in years, Durga felt happy and blessed for all the knowledge she had about plants. The news from her grandmother that her father was 'better than the week before' pepped her up further.

Jeena had only one worry. "What'll happen to all this

when Mrs. Roberts comes back?"

"She won't. Abhik and I have sent out an email with details of all the financial irregularities to all the Board Members. They have agreed to send her a firing notice and install you as the General Manager of this place. You will get a salary and living quarters," assured Durga

Jeena was ecstatic.

"Something needs to be done. That idiotic Durga is suddenly so popular just because she and her friends are doing some work there, and the servants whose relatives are holed up there are spreading all this information in the school. It's like they have become some kind of heroes. I need a plan to bring them down. I am fed up of getting no help from you, Jug and Lizzy— I am only friends with you because I choose to. I can always choose someone else," threatened Akanksha, carelessly falling onto her bed. Had it not been for her father's insistence, she would not have come here. In particular, she disliked Principal Roy, who she suspected had a soft corner for Durga and her gang.

An only daughter, Akanksha was spoilt beyond reason and comprehension as she announced it herself, as though it was some sort of definitive advantage. What she wanted to get, she got. Now, her mind, body, heart, and soul were focused on hurting Durga.

She also knew that her family was related to Durga.

Though Durga was unaware of this, Akanksha was privy to her own parents' conversations about how they quite 'undeservedly' got 'everything' after the adoption, while their family, even though royal by birth, had never been considered.

They are just pavement thrash. Nothing more. I will get her! simmered Akanksha inwardly.

"Yes, Akanksha. We will certainly think of something," muttered Jagannath, unsure of what to say. He found Akanksha's vindication quite annoying, but chose not to say anything.

Elizabeth shared Jagannath's sentiments. They both stuck to Akanksha out of a sheer sense of loyalty. When they were being bullied, Akanksha rescued them. While with her, nobody dared to try those tricks on them ever again.

Akanksha looked at both of them shrewdly. She knew in her heart that Jagannath was not conniving enough and that Elizabeth was super straight. She would have to think of something.

It was already evening. Though Akanksha shared the room with Elizabeth, the room was literally a reflection of what Akanksha wanted. Elizabeth was relegated to a corner. Her study table had many decorative items: a portrait of her parents framed in gold, a vase of fresh flowers, a decanter filled with an infusion of fruits, two flasks, each containing a different type of energy drink, and a fish bowl filled with potpourri. Come rain or sunshine, Akanksha trained rigorously.

"Okay, then. Will see you tomorrow," waved Jagannath, almost glad to escape.

Akanksha inclined her head.

Elizabeth also moved to her corner of the room and started settling in.

A knock on the door made Elizabeth scamper towards the door. As a rule, Akanksha never answered the door. A package came in for Akanksha.

Akanksha's eyes shone as she hurriedly ripped open the delicate packaging to reveal a stunning cream-white Dior prom gown with a lace-fitted bodice, full skirt, and a high neckline. Hugging the dress, she ran to a large floor-length mirror to check it out.

Elizabeth sighed.

"Wow, Dior, Lizzy, did you see that? It looks lovely. And look at these silver necklaces that go so well with the dress and shoes! So thoughtful! Gosh, gotta call mom!"

Elizabeth nodded admiringly.

Akanksha flung the dress on the bed and called her mother.

"Mummy, thank you! I got the present, and it's lovely! The necklaces and shoes are a perfect match. Just in time for the Spring Ball at school. Are you coming? Uh-huh... it's okay, mom. I will manage. Bye...ciao."

Akanksha flung her mobile on the bed. Elizabeth was startled. "That's it! I got a perfect idea! Let's do the same thing but better! Help the kids in the center with medicine and clean up the place. And I will be the cynosure of all eyes at the spring ball with this dress! That shabby wretch Durga is always watching me with envy. She has no style!" exclaimed Akanksha.

"Absolutely brill, Akku," resonated Elizabeth mechanically. As long as Akanksha was busy scheming, she would be saved from her constant belittling.

"Good. Let me work on my skin schedule while you catch up on your science. Remember, we have only five months to go for the Science Quiz," Akanksha nodded in Elizabeth's direction, who retreated to her corner.

It was Saturday night. All the students were studying exam materials together in the common room.

"God, I am beat! We need to get some winks. When the body is deprived of sleep, it will cause stress. What good would that do to us?" complained Janice dramatically. Everyone nodded sleepily. The time was nearly 10:30 PM. According to school regulations, they had to be in bed by midnight, but rules were flexed a bit during exam time.

"Wish we had something to rejuvenate…" complained Durga.

"Like what, Madam? Nectar?" grunted Keith.

"You mean Soma..." quipped Janice.

Everyone burst out laughing.

Suddenly, they saw a lady staff member come in abruptly and stand before Durga, tears streaming from her eyes.

"What is the matter, Satemma auntie? Tell me," asked Durga in Telugu.

"Amma, Durgamma, my daughter is at Rainbow Home where Akankshamma gave her some medicine, and she has fallen sick. Can you help, please? I heard you helped a lot of people at the old age home. I will be ever grateful to you."

Janice, Keith, and Abhik gathered around.

"Sure, can we call the center now? Is it too late?"

"No, my brother is working there; he can make a video call," Satemma said.

"Good, good, let's talk to him right now!"

Durga talked to Gopi, the in-charge of Rainbow Orphanage, which also served as a hostel for kids from underprivileged communities. The center charged a small fee to care for children whose parents were daily wage workers.

Durga completed the call and talked to Satemma, consoling her.

“Satemma auntie, it’s nothing but a small stomach upset. I have asked Gopi to give her the right medicine. She will be okay.”

Satemma mutely fell at Durga’s feet.

“Hey, this is not necessary! Don’t worry, I will check what’s going on there,” assured Durga as Satemma left, looking cheerful again.

“What happened, D?” asked Abhik.

“It’s funny, really. But not so funny! You know what our heroine Akanksha has been doing at the Rainbow Center? Trying to force feed them some herb powders! Gopi told me that the inmates are coming down with all sorts of complaints.”

“Seriously? What’s wrong with her? She’s trying to imitate you, for God’s sake!” laughed Janice.

“Let’s create a podcast on this and push it into Blast On!” suggested Keith.

“Yes, I will see to it that it’s done anonymously,” smiled Abhik smugly.

“Guys…we will see you in the morning…Good night,” Keith and Abhik left.

As they snuggled in their beds, Durga remembered the chance remark about Soma.

Soma, did it ever exist? She wondered. *Well, seems like a myth.* Shrugging the thought off, she fell asleep.

"Do-gooder at work makes people sick!"

Abhik's 'anonymous' podcast went viral on Blast On! Akanksha and her team were livid. But since Abhik had covered his tracks so well, there needed to be proof. But the damage was done. Akanksha was slipping in her popularity.

Durga somehow felt bad for Akanksha. On her request, Abhik retracted the podcast reluctantly. Janice and Keith were relieved, too.

Meanwhile, they had the second part of the detention waiting for them — the 'Clean the Vodarevu beach' activity. On arrival, they saw the beach littered with plastic wrappers, cups, discarded clothing, and garbage.

"Guys, let's get this beach sparkling clean, and we will set an example. Let's think," said Janice, and they all agreed wholeheartedly.

Durga, Janice, Keith, and Abhik brainstormed and devised an idea.

This time, Abhik proposed a 'Citizen Awareness Campaign' which called on people's support in beach cleaning. With colorful and thoughtful videos and pictures of them in action on the beach storming the Internet, their beach-cleaning efforts gained momentum. Friends, neighbors, fishermen, children, and even some small-time film stars volunteered their time by connecting with Durga and team on the social networks. People began gathering for weekly Sunday afternoon clean-ups to participate in what they called *A date with the Blue.*

Their efforts paid off after four weeks. A 4-km stretch of the beach where families gathered regularly every evening looked much cleaner. Abhik estimated that they had moved at least 10 tonnes of plastic and garbage altogether. The crowning moment was when the Chief Minister heard about the effort and came down personally to the beach to 'join in the effort of school children,' which made headlines in all local dailies.

The Blast On! carried many stories of the super successful beach clean-up. Durga, Janice, Keith, and Abhik became as popular as film stars, on the campus.

Chapter Nine

Dead Body No.2

It was time for lunch. Janice, Abhik, and Keith had decided to go early to the cafeteria to block a table. Durga remained thoughtful as she wandered back to her room to pick up her mobile charger before reminding Abhik to keep up his research on Adrian Gerber.

Her mobile trilled.

Durga was surprised to see her grandmother calling. She always maintained very well-planned timelines to call her.

Worried, Durga picked up her call.

"Amma, how are you?"

Her grandmother's calm voice came over the phone.

"Everything is super fine, Bamma. How's dad? And mom? Any improvement in Dad?"

"Well, he's better, but his memory has not returned. Your mom is fully back to action."

"That's good to hear. Bamma, what is it that you wanted to talk about?" asked Durga intuitively.

Two seconds of silence ensued.

"Well, I don't want to rattle you, but our staff member Pushpa died this morning. Anyways it will make the news, so I am telling you first."

"Whaaat? How? Was she sick?"

"She was found murdered. She was outside in an unusual locality, too! I somehow never thought Pushpa had anything to do with such places!" Durga could hear her grandmother sighing.

"My God, that's horrible news. How did this happen?"

"I don't know, Talli. The Police are investigating. Don't trouble yourself. We will handle it. Meanwhile, why don't you come home this weekend along with your friends?"

"Yes, Bamma," Durga said distractedly.

Durga sat thinking.

Another murder. First, Dr. Uwe and now Pushpa. Cheerful, rotund, very spick, and span Pushpa! Why?

Durga felt sad for Pushpa.

Lady working at Gajendrapatiraju's family mansion found murdered! screamed the next day's papers.

Durga sighed. They were all back at the Devdi for the weekend, which was extended because of a local festival. But the atmosphere was somber.

Abhik was still furiously researching Adrian. Keith sipped an iced mango milkshake. Janice was trying her hand at Sudoku.

Durga was pacing up and down.

“Guys, I seriously think we need to find more details about Pushpa’s death. I feel its our duty.”

All of them sat still.

“Solve a murder. Are you kidding?” asked Keith.

“Yes, D, I agree. I somehow think it’s important to solve this mystery. Let’s do this,” suggested Abhik decisively.

Janice jumped in.

“I think so, too, Diggy. My blood is boiling that such a dreadful thing could happen to Pushpa. We must at least try.”

“Yes, Jenny. I am glad you guys are with me.”

“It’s a good idea, but where do we begin? What happens if we get caught?” asked Keith nervously.

“Well, let’s cross that bridge when we have to. Best not to overthink,” said Janice.

All of them smiled.

“Let’s begin then. What do we know about this lady Pushpa?” asked Janice.

“Give me a few minutes, and I will tell you,” said Abhik,

and everyone watched, entranced as he whipped out his laptop and started typing furiously with a single hand.

"Let me hack into the staff details of the facility management company that maintains your property. It's called 'Shine Housekeeping and Facility Services.' I noticed the logo on the uniforms. I'm in. Let's see...Pushpalata Bulusu. Age 32, originally a resident of Siddipet. Educated in the local Government High School, discontinued after 7th grade, came to work for Shine about seven years ago. Can speak two languages. No family. Satisfactory conduct. Hmm, now let's check the police verification details..."

They all checked the screen of his laptop, which was downloading the National Crime Records Bureau."Yeah...it's here. Pushpalata Bulusu...aha, interesting. She does have a petty theft to her credit!! She was in a Juvenile Center for one year but was released for good behavior," summed up Abhik triumphantly.

"So Pushpa is a former criminal?" asked Keith incredulously.

"But, we must not judge too harshly. We don't know the circumstances she was in at that time. Here, Pushpa was always dependable and trustworthy," said Durga.

"I wouldn't be so sure. I hacked into her bank account and found that Pushpa received large sums of money, sometimes up to one lakh rupees, from an unconnected account over the last two years. So, Pushpa was up to something!" declared Abhik.

"Wow, Abhi, you are a genius," exclaimed Durga. "Yes," murmured all the others.

"That I am, kiddos. Now, let's see if we can snoop around her room and see if we can find some details?" suggested Abhik.

"Do you think that's even possible?" asked Keith.

"Yes, of course. Keith. I know where her room was. So yes, we can go there," said Durga.

"But how will we go there without anyone noticing us? We will most certainly look very out of place going there," asked Keith.

"We don't need to go physically..." Abhik's mischievous eyes twinkled, enjoying the looks on their miffed faces.

"Well, I will put a small camera on anyone who can go there...like another staff member?" suggested Abhik.

Durga thought for a moment and smiled.

"Well, I will need to take Suma into confidence. She's my handmaid, quite innocent, really. We can ask her to go surreptitiously and plant the camera on her. I will call her." Durga rang a bell.

"Wow, Princess Power at play," grunted Keith admiringly.

A thin, bright-eyed girl with a long plait and a grey uniform presented herself, bowing deeply to Durga.

“Come here,” beckoned Durga gently.

Suma approached shyly. Durga whispered something in her ears. Suma nodded in understanding.

Abhik rummaged through his laptop pouch and handed her a small button camera device. Suma attached it to her outfit discretely, and casually made her way towards the servant’s quarters.

“Tracking...Suma is near the cottage where Pushpa had lived. She’s only a few steps away...” Abhik launched into a running commentary, as the camera device was giving an excellent video capture.

All of them gathered around Abhik’s laptop.

“If anyone asks, say we are watching a movie,” forewarned Durga. All of them nodded.

On reaching Pushpa’s quarters, Suma made sure there was no one around, and softly inserted a key from the master key bunch she always carried with her into the keyhole. She carefully stepped inside and closed the door behind her.

It was a spacious enough room. Steel engravings of random subjects hung on the walls with one or two calendars sporting images of gods. An untidy bed and a great deal of bric-a-brac were scattered haphazardly around the room. There was a large old suitcase filled with clothes. As Suma riffled around, there were many nice-looking clothes (probably hand-me-downs), a brush, comb, an old, dented silver-backed mirror, a bank passbook, and a faded newspaper wrapped around a small Ganesha statue.

Suma held up the passbook for Abhik to click a picture of the details. Nothing else seemed to be of interest. Just as Suma was about to close the briefcase, Durga's eyes caught sight of a small, folded newspaper piece jutting out of a pocket.

"Suma, take the paper, close the briefcase, and come away as quietly and quickly as possible," commanded Durga. Suma nodded nervously, put everything back as it was, opened the door, and quietly exited. Just as she was about to turn the corner, she and they saw a team of Police officers in khakis accompanied by Krishna Murthy, the Estate Manager going towards Pushpa's quarters. Suma slipped away noiselessly.

"Hey, great job Abhi. Now, see this. This piece of newspaper is rectangular and cut out of the middle page. The heading says, *Man caught for house burglary.* There is a photo of the thief, too. This dates back ten years! Can you enlarge this and Google the details?" asked Durga.

"Hold on! Yes. This one's name is Appala Narsimham. He was sentenced to three years' rigorous imprisonment for robbing houses," said Abhik.

"Well, no clues there. Check if you can find out from where the money was deposited into her bank account, if possible?" asked Durga.

"Sure, I am checking...here, I hacked into her bank's

server and found that the transfer was made from an account with only two words in the description. That means someone covered their tracks well," said Abhik.

"Can you dig further and find out the details of the person who transferred the one lakh rupees to Pushpa?"

"Yes, D, give me a few minutes..." Abhik's fingers raced on the keyboard.

"Aha, I am getting better and better at this! Here, I found the details. They belong to a person called T. Krishna Murthy, a resident of Visakhapatnam."

"Why would he send any money to Pushpa?" asked Janice

"Maybe he's related to her in some way, a long-lost cousin, brother?" suggested Keith.

All fell silent.

"Let me see the paper clipping again. The face looks familiar somehow. I wish we had a clearer picture," murmured Durga.

"Well, I do have an app that cleans up blurry photos. Hold on, it's uploading… well, here is the person!" finished Abhik exultantly.

"Oh my God, that is our Estate Manager — Krishna Murthy. So, he is Appala Narasimham, the known criminal?" an astonished Durga bluttered.

"This means maybe Pushpa found his secret and was blackmailing him. Finally, he felt scared and killed her?" suggested Abhik.

Durga nodded.

"This also means my entire family is in some sort of danger, Abhi," said Durga slowly.

"Shall we tell Bamma?" asked Janice anxiously.

Durga didn't say anything.

"Actually, why did he come into service with our family? There must be another reason. Maybe he's even responsible for the accident of my parents? After all, he's the one who fixes their itineraries, drivers..." Durga trailed off.

"Oh my God, this is indeed a dangerous situation. What must we do?"

"Abhi, just hack into Krishna Murthy's phone records," said Durga.

"What are you looking for, D?"

"I don't exactly know, Abhi."

"Let's see. His phone records will be filled with the names of your family, staff, and those who work for you. How can you ever work through that maze? In any case, here you are..."

"Thanks, Abhi. Let me see," Durga took the laptop from Abhik and started scrolling down the numbers.

She stopped at one name.

"Dhyaneshwara Raju? Akanksha's father? Why would our Estate Manager be talking to him? What is the connection?" Durga wondered.

The atmosphere in the house remained solemn. Durga went to see her mother and father. Her father seemed very nearly normal, physically. But no light of love came into his eyes when he saw Durga. How she missed that! Her mother hugged her.

"How are things with you, Kanna? I haven't talked to you for so long!" Durga's mother sounded calm.

"Amma, don't worry, everything is okay. How are you feeling now?"

"Much better. I think I will be back to normal by tomorrow,"

They both sat quietly for a few moments.

"Amma, how did this happen? Do you remember any of it?" asked Durga.

"Not much, actually. It's still such a shock. One moment everything was okay. And then in the next, something hit us. I don't remember anything after that until I woke up in the hospital. By the way, I have to tell you. I must go away to Visakhapatnam on some urgent business. Bamma asked me to get it done."

Durga jumped up.

"What? Now? No, I won't allow this," she said rebelliously.

"Wait, Talli. Listen to me first. Now that you have been coronated, you must know that a part of our extended family is trying to prove us as ineligible for the crown. I must sort this out with the lawyers."

"Is it Dhyaneshwara Raju?"

Her mother looked shocked!

"How do you know?"

"A lucky guess?"

"Well, I will sort out all the documentation once and for all. Meanwhile, Nanna will undergo treatment. There is no other solution," said her mother decisively.

Thoughtfully, Durga walked over to her grandmother's room, knocked, and entered.

Her grandmother was sitting at her desk, punching out a message on her laptop. She looked up as Durga approached her. She closed the laptop and held out her arms.

"Come, Amma."

Durga hugged her grandmother, and settled down in a chair close to her.

"Are you comfortable? Is there anything to ask me?"

"Yes, Bamma."

"What's on your mind, Amma?"

How to tell you, Bamma? There are so many treacherous people around?

"Do you trust Mr. Krishna Murthy?"

"Well, yes, He has been around for a long time. But lately, he has been acting very irresponsibly. He's once again on leave for two weeks. Why did you ask?"

"Nothing Bamma. Just like that."

Both were silent for a few minutes.

"Bamma, can Dhyaneshwara Raju prove me ineligible for the crown?" blurted Durga.

Probably, for the first time ever, she saw her grandmother's eyes flash with anger.

"Hmm, how did you come to that conclusion?"

"Well, Amma told me she's going to Visakhapatnam. By the way, his daughter is my classmate."

Her grandmother stood up abruptly and went to the window.

Durga worried that she may have offended her grandmother.

"Bamma, I am sorry. Was it a wrong question to ask?"

Her grandmother paused.

"Well, it's time, you knew anyway. Dhyaneshwara Raju is your father's cousin and your uncle. When Rajasaheb, your grandfather, decided to anoint your father as the King, Dhyana was very upset. But then, there are complex reasons why your father was chosen. I will explain it to you one day. After the coronation, Dhyana decided to split from the family. That's why he dropped our family name too. For years, his jealousy and anger simmered, and he made contact through lawyers, sending us legal notices about how this coronation was invalid. It didn't work. I know that he will never give up."

"So, if something happens to Nanna, would he be the King?"

Queen Mother turned around and looked straight into Durga's eyes.

She's so regal! Will I ever be like her? Durga wondered.

"No, Amma. I made sure of that by conducting your coronation. You are now the legal successor and the heir to the throne. No one can take your place. What a coincidence that his daughter is your classmate. A very big coincidence indeed!" added her grandmother thoughtfully.

Chapter Ten

Murder Mystery Deepens

Durga found her friends at the pool. They had left a note for her. All of them were swimming and taking selfies. They waved as she approached. Durga joined her friends for a swim. Abhik loved swimming. He swam longer and harder than anyone else. It was a fantastic sight for them to see how he managed to slither off and on to his wheelchair. He never asked for their assistance ever. After swimming, they sipped on some juice and sat watching the sunset in complete silence. It was a mesmerizing sight. For the first time in days, Durga felt refreshed.

"Okay, D. Spill the beans, please. You look too thoughtful. Any news?" implored Keith.

"It's Dhyaneshwara Raju."

"Isn't that our enemy's father?" Keith asked.

"Yes, he is my uncle and next in line to the throne. Since I have been coronated, he no longer has any claim. So, there is your motive. He may have planted Krishna Murthy as our Manager to study everything and everyone. That could be the only explanation, and when Pushpa found out his secret somehow, Krishna Murthy would have tried to bribe her from telling Bamma. When she refused, he may have killed her. This could be an accident too, we can't be sure. I now think my uncle may be responsible for my parents' accident also. He would have assumed that with my father dead, he would be crowned King, as I am a girl. He may not have expected two things — that my father would live and that my grandmother would decide to make me the heir to the throne!"

All of them were quiet for a while.

"Maybe, there is more to Pushpa than we figured. Abhi, you had already hacked her phone records. What were the last five calls she made before she died," asked Durga.

Abhik took out his laptop with a flourish and started typing furiously.

"Yes, of the last five calls three were to your house. Two were to different numbers — one, to Chamalapalle village, close to a location about 50 km from here. The last one is probably a spam call," said Abhik.

"I think we should take a look at her briefcase again. I will call Suma," declared Durga.

"What are you looking for, D?"

"I am not sure, Abhi. Just a hunch."

Having pinned the camera on, Suma once again made her way towards the staff quarters. The area was deserted. She slipped into Pushpa's room and opened the briefcase.

"Is there anything else, like a small box or a purse?"

Rummaging through the briefcase, Suma found a black velvet drawstring purse within which were a mini diary and a small device.

A few moments later, all of them were staring at their find. The mini diary had some numbers scribbled randomly in it.

"Wow, D, there is something very queer here," murmured Abhik excitedly.

They all looked at Abhik, whose eyes were sparkling.

"This is a very advanced device. It's not your usual type!"

"What do you mean, Abhi?"

"D, we are dealing with something very complicated. Give me the diary."

"These numbers are scrambled and codes of some sort, probably for communication. This means..." Abhik stopped doubtfully, mid-sentence.

"What is it? God, this suspense is making me cray-cray," muttered Janice.

"Well, Jenny, this can mean only one thing. Pushpa was

not your usual everyday staff member. She is...I mean, she was a spy!"

For one full minute, nobody said anything.

"That makes two! Krishna Murthy, and now this one! How many more spies are roaming freely in my home?" Durga looked utterly flabbergasted.

"Understandable, but these are the facts."

"Abhi, can you find out more about this device and the markings in the diary? One more thing...the last call she made may not be a spam call at all! If we can get some details about it, we could get more clues."

"Will do, D."

Durga lay in her soft bed holding her old stuffed teddy, Sparkle. She had had it since she was three years old. Only her mother knew this secret. Durga smiled as memories of her mother chasing her all over the garden came to her mind. She missed her mom. Her mobile trilled, and she saw a message from Abhik.

Come.

Durga got up and rushed to the herb garden. It had become a place for all of them to meet by tacit agreement.

"Well, I researched this gadget in as many databases, and I finally came up with nothing!"

"Ohhh…"

Abhik waved away a wail of dejected voices.

"Hold on, and the game is not over yet! It's just beginning!"

"Ah, Abhi, can you please cut the theatrics out and come to the point?"

Like a well-organized magician, he flourished his laptop screen and shouted, "*Ta-da*"

All the faces turned eagerly towards the laptop screen.

There seemed to be nothing there — just a bunch of graphics and some numbers.

"Well, I just discovered that this device is not ordinary. It's highly customized. I say this because of its sheer parameters. But having hacked into some very advanced databases, I found that this one belongs to a company — Seltenheit GmbH. The company is based out of Cologne, Germany. The company specializes in selling plants in rare varieties that are hard to find elsewhere. The proprietors are Adrian Gerber and Van den Bosch."

"Wow, so there is a connection! Abhi, you are awesome!" exclaimed Durga.

Einstein. Eureka. Screamed Nibbles.

Janice scowled.

“Alright, alrighty, cool it, dude. Now, let us get back to the brass tacks. What does this mean?”

Durga was silent for a moment.

“Well, I think I know. If Adrian and his thugs specialize in rare plants, they must be stealing them from India. Was Pushpa working for them? Was she responsible for my parents’ accident? Why was KM paying her?”

“Well, where is that diary? That might offer us some clues,” Abhik said.

Janice fetched the journal. The entries were made mostly by date and the activity on that day.

“Let’s see what she was doing on the day she died,” said Durga.

The diary entry read —

Got the money from KM. With this, freedom, finally!

“Well, what a coincidence.”

“I don’t think this was meant as that sort of freedom. Maybe it was a financial problem? She was paying off some loan or something?” said Durga.

“Aha, I found an essential detail about Pushpa.”

Adrian was still working on his laptop. They all gathered around him.

“She was regularly sending money to a lady. But since

we know she was an orphan, I wondered who this lady might be. It turns out she is her cousin sister. They must have been close in their childhood."

"Wow! How did you find this?"

"Simple, I hacked into her bank accounts."

"Uh-huh, isn't all this checking dangerous, Abhi?' asked Durga worriedly.

"Nope. I clear my tracks when I return; in any case, most of the systems in India are so outdated. Nothing would ever come back to me, even if I did leave something. That's for sure."

"Okay. Meanwhile, would it help to visit her sister once and get additional details about her?" asked Janice.

"That's a good idea. Let's put that device back in her suitcase so that KM doesn't get suspicious. Also, keep a small camera device near Pushpa's room. This way we can keep an eye on things!"

"That's a good strategy," approved Abhik.

Just then, Suma came in and bowed.

Durga, springing up, handed the device to Suma and instructed her to put it back.

"Your Highness, Queen Mother requests your presence."

"Okay, coming! Guys, will be back shortly."

"Amma, I wish that all of you visit Pushpa's cousin who lives in the neighboring village. I have a gift for her as well. Assure her of our support. Since Krishna Murthy is on leave I will send Suma and Security Officer Rajendra Singh with you. Seshachalam will drive you there,"

"I would love to, Bamma," Durga couldn't contain her enthusiasm.

"Guys, let's go. Bamma asked us to meet Pushpa's cousin in the village!"

"Great! Let's go."

They all filed towards the main entrance.

Rajendra Singh saluted smartly, with a click of his heels.

Driver Seshachalam had brought out the two BMWs. In 15 minutes, they arrived at the location.

The cottage where Pushpa's cousin Radha lived was only a few steps from the bus stop. It was a small cottage. Two children were playing on the doorstep. One was eating a biscuit, and the other was shouting and beating on the door with a tin tray. Abhik decided to stay in the car.

Durga, Janice, and Keith knocked on the door.

A woman in a multi-colored saree and untidy hair

opened the door. She screamed at the children, who didn't seem to listen to her at all.

She bowed to Durga and went down to touch her feet. Durga caught her midways to see tears streaming down her cheeks.

"Radhamma, it's okay. Have courage. We will take care of you."

The lady nodded and welcomed them into the small cottage.

It was sparse but clean.

Radha spread a mat for them to sit on.

Durga handed over a package to Radha. It contained some money.

Meanwhile, Rajendra Singh deposited three months' groceries in the kitchen.

Radha made a grateful gesture.

"Radhamma, were you and Pushpa very close?" asked Durga in Telugu.

"Yes, Yuvarani Saheba. Our fathers were brothers, and we all lived in the same house. However, Pushpa's parents passed away after a sudden illness. Then Pushpa was sent to an orphanage. But we had a strong bond. She would visit me at least once in two years. After she started working at Rani Saheba's household, she supported my family and me. My husband left many jobs, but we were okay since she always cared for us. Now I don't know about our future!" Once again, Radha's eyes welled up with tears.

Durga sat next to Radha and put her hand around her.

"Don't worry, Radhamma, Rani Sahiba will care for you. Did Pushpa live with you when she came home?"

"Yes. Pushpa kept some things in a room at the back. Sometimes, she would come in at odd times."

"Can we see her room?"

"Of course, Yuvarani Saheba. It's right there," pointed Radha.

Durga, Janice, and Keith circled to the back and stepped into the room.

It was very small. There was one bed. Underneath the bed was a large suitcase.

Radhamma left them and hurried into the kitchen to make some tea.

Janice went down on all fours, pulled the suitcase out, and started rummaging through it. In it was a small-sized laptop. Janice held it out to Keith, who quickly slid it into his backpack. There was nothing else of importance in the room. They pushed the suitcase back in its place and came back to sit on the mat.

Radhamma brought some tea and biscuits. They sipped the tea and munched the biscuits. Radha was looking more cheerful than she did when they arrived. Finally, they said their goodbyes and left.

Once in the car, Keith handed over the laptop to Abhik. Within minutes, he had downloaded all its contents.

"Okay, Abhi, let's hear it!" Janice was already making ferocious faces at Abhik, who was keying away smugly.

Durga, Janice, and Keith were watching curiously.

"Ah, oki...oki. I figured it all out. She was definitely a spy!"

"Any other details?" asked Durga

"Well, she was probably reporting to Adrian Gerber!"

On reaching the Devdi, they settled down on the terrace, watching the sunset, sipping icy mint-lemon sodas and cookies arranged thoughtfully by the Chef.

After a spell, they went back to their rooms to rest.

Durga went to see her father.

The dinner gong rang. It was sharp eight, and they all hurried towards the dining room.

As usual, Queen Mother was already seated.

"I heard the day went well. I am very thankful to you and also proud of you!"

A happy smile spread across their faces.

Chapter Eleven

Herb Garden Triggers A Thought

"Guys, have you seen the message from school? We have extended holidays. We have one more full week!" exclaimed Keith happily. He was enjoying his time at the Devdi. Janice was jumping and squealing. Abhik looked radiant. Queen Mother had thoughtfully arranged portable ramps for his wheelchair at essential points on the property, giving Abhik the freedom to move about the whole place on his own.

The four friends sat in the lush herb garden with pretty water fountains cascading over rock wall terraces. Some pathways and stairs led to a small knoll-like elevation. Picnic chairs with canopies offered a vantage view of the entire garden. There were themed herb beds, each of which had about 20-30 species. The Indian Ayurveda Garden, which was the largest, had many species such as Ashwagandha, Amla fruit trees, Patchouly, Lemon, Palma Rosa Grasses, and, of course, Tulsi or Basil.

To the other side was the Fragrance Garden that featured a lily pond and a rose-climber arch with several scented aromatherapy herbs such as Jasmine, Helichrysum, Vetiver, Patchouli, Spikenard, and many types of Lavenders.

Then there was the Culinary Garden with the Chef's favorites — Italian Oregano, Bronze Fennel, Mexican Marigold, Vietnamese Coriander, and Stevia, which is many times sweeter than sugar.

The friends sat sipping iced lemon tea. The food array included orange and spice-pureed carrots, grilled tofu, and raspberry angel fruit cake. The fragrance of the herb garden was very stimulating. The weather was perfect too. Not very warm or cold. Slightly cloudy.

Raindrops falling on my head, Nibbles was singing.

"Greetings to Princess Durgavathi. Her Highness, Queen Mother, would like to see you all in the library. Thank you."

"Thank you, Suma. We will be there in a few minutes," murmured Durga. Suma bowed and left.

Wordlessly, they filed one after another to the library.

As they entered, they saw Queen Mother sitting in a lounge chair near the large window overlooking the herb garden, reading a book. She smiled as they approached her.

"Good to see you. How are you all doing?"

"All well, Bamma," they chorused in unison.

"Please sit. I have an assignment for you. Our Master Chef, Virupaksha, has asked if you might enjoy spending time harvesting herbs in the herb garden. The experience is a very enriching one! By the way, our Chef is a Ph.D. in nutrition and has great knowledge of culinary cultures from around the world."

"Oh, we would love that, Bamma!"

"Wow, good idea!"

"Super-duper... love the concept!"

Queen Mother smiled at their enthusiasm.

"Very good. That's settled, then. Please remember, it's a full day's job. Chef will guide you and help you with the required implements once you go to the kitchens. Your lunch will be served in the garden today."

"Thank you, Bamma. We will certainly enjoy the experience," gushed Durga as they all ran towards the kitchen.

Chef Virupaksha welcomed them all.

"Greetings, Princess Durgavathi. Very glad to see you and your honorable friends here."

"Chef, please, no need for too many formalities. We are here as students and would like to learn everything we can about the job today."

"Very well. Thank you, Princess. We will harvest

different types of herbs, which we do from time to time, and store them. Please come here."

The Chef walked them to the long table where various shiny instruments like shears, scissors, sharp cutting tools, garden gloves, and aprons were spread out.

"You can pick up your tools. My assistant, Shyam will be with you to guide you. I will arrange the lunch in the garden. Would you like some Italian? Pizza, perhaps?"

"Yes, Thank you, Chef,"

"Okay then, let's get to work. Shyam, you can accompany them to the herb garden."

"Please be sure you don't remove more than 1/3 of the plant's leaves or stems at a time. Take the sharp cutting tool with long blades that fits very well into those tiny spaces where stems and leaves meet so that you can make a clean, precise, quick-healing cut. Harvest the bottom leaves before the upper ones. Younger leaves are more flavorful, tender, and less bitter. Always wipe the blade after use. For chives and sage, cut off the stems from the outside of the plant, starting about a half-inch above the base. You can pinch Sage leaves off individually," Chef Shyam gave a very elaborate session before they got to work.

"This is great," sighed Durga. Janice nodded. Abhik and Keith were enjoying themselves too.

Together they harvested large amounts of herbs like basil, cilantro, dill, oregano, parsley, chives, sage, and thyme in the color-coded baskets.

Before they knew it, it was lunchtime. They washed up and gathered at the table in the garden enthusiastically. Chef outdid himself again. There were four different kinds of large pan pizzas. A family-style caesar salad, garlic bread, a citrus, fennel and avocado salad, mozzarella bites, and a large green monster salad, were the side dishes. The dessert trolley was even more enticing. A selection of ice creams — chocolate, vanilla, peppermint, fruit-flavored sorbets in pineapple, lemon, and berry flavors, and a cinnamon streusel dessert pizza loaded with cinnamon, sugar, and butter made for the eye-popping array.

"Ah-ah, I am going to put on 20 kilos. I am eating like a pig," groaned Abhik, who had a soft spot for sweets.

"Right again, Pardner," sighed Keith.

Chef Virupaksha presented himself, and they all thanked him profusely.

"Thank you. Post lunch, you will harvest the Indian herbs. I have one request. Tonight, you will eat a traditional Indian dinner and understand the role of plant-based nutrition in our ancient culinary culture."

"Thank you, Chef. We are so eager to listen to you!" said Abhik. All of them nodded.

After lunch, they all went back to their rooms for some

rest. They had to gather back in the Indian herb garden for the post-lunch activity.

Durga went to see her father. He was reading a book. He looked at her, nodded, and smiled as she approached him. *Oh Nanna, where are you? I miss you!* Silently, she sat near him and held his hand. He seemed content enough to allow it. For a while, they sat together. Bamma had assured her that he was being treated with the best therapies. A thought was forming in her head, and fast. She would find a cure!

She got up and waved goodbye. Her father did the same.

Durga rushed back to her room. She opened the safe, and got the copper plates, and her father's journal.

Was there anything for reviving memory?

She hurriedly scanned her father's journal and saw the herb Brahmi — Centella Asiatica (Centella) — a perennial herb from the Apiaceae family. Brahmi was considered a tonic for the brain as it improves brain power by preventing damage caused by free radicals, improves cognition, and helps to make the memory sharp and clear. The number against this herb was 21. Durga immediately referred to the Melakarta chart she had saved in her phone. The raga was Keeravani.

Durga sang a composition in the raga, and a copper plate sprang open. According to the plate, the ideal way of taking Brahmi was to add its powder in milk and drink it.

Durga found the jar that contained some dried Brahmi herbs in it. She put everything back into the box, and locked it in her safe.

She powdered the herb, put it in a small sachet, and rushed to the kitchen. She asked the Chef for a glass of milk and took it to her father's room.

He was still reading. He gave a small smile as she approached him. Durga took out the sachet of Brahmi powder, mixed it in milk, and gave it to him. He took it and drank it.

After that, Durga went to see the Chef in the kitchen.

"Greetings Princess, you should have asked for me, and I would have come. Why did you take the trouble of coming down to the kitchens?"

"Chef, thank you. It's okay. I need you to do something, please. I want you to give Brahmi powder with milk to Nanna every day at night."

"Surely, Princess. We will follow your command diligently," assured the Chef. His eyes shone with kindness and admiration.

Durga thanked the Chef and left.

Her mobile buzzed.

We are in the garden.

Luckily, the day was a bit cloudy and enjoyable. It was almost 3:30 PM when they gathered back in the Indian herb garden to continue with the harvesting. Chef Shyam accompanied them as they went around the aromatic garden feeling light-headed.

They found many interesting herbs such as Ashwagandha, Brahmi, Cumin, Turmeric, Licorice root, Ginseng, Snake Jasmine and Stevia, Arrowroot, Shankhpushpi, Kushmanda, Banana on Rocks, Vacha, though not of Indian origin. Chef Shyam explained how herbs had many medicinal uses and were a part of Indian traditional cuisine.

It was late evening by the time they wrapped up the harvesting. They had some refreshing mint tea and spicy biscuits in the garden.

"I saved some of the herbs, which might be useful for us, D," said Janice.

"Well done, Jenny," said Durga.

"Let's sundry and gather them in small bottles. They might come in handy some day," said Keith.

They went back to their rooms to get refreshed and gather for dinner at eight.

Durga, Janice, Keith, and Abhik strolled towards the dining hall.

On Bamma's advice, they all wore Indian attires.

Queen Mother came in, and they all took some selfies.

Staff in dhotis with gold borders and turbans started filling the table with many delicious dishes.

Once Queen Mother was seated, they all sat at the table.

Chef Virupaksha came in and bowed respectfully to Queen Mother and turned towards them.

"Good evening. Today, I want to explain the importance of Indian culinary culture, which has rich and diverse plant-based cuisines. Food is an important milestone of religious and social identity, with varying preferences, which has also driven different sections of the population to innovate extensively with food sources, especially with vegetables. Can you guess how many Indians are vegetarians?"

"Yes, about 31%?" answered Abhik.

"Spot on! There is a context to this. Many recipes may have emerged during the initial Vedic period. In ancient times, vegetarianism was actively encouraged as a part of social, cultural, and religious practices," said Chef Virupaksha.

"Nowadays, thanks to advanced technologies, we eat fruits and vegetables all through the year. So what is the significance of eating seasonal fruits and vegetables?" asked Durga.

"An excellent question! Undoubtedly, food culture in

India emphasizes eating agricultural and natural produce 'in season.' For example, our own vakkai, Carissa carandas, mangoes, and locally sourced greens like bachali or menthi during the summer, pumpkins during the rainy monsoon months, and bulbs and tubers during the winter months were all used in cooking. This emphasis was based on a cultural practice that in-season foods are more potent, tastier, and have more excellent nutritional value. It is still true. Research now suggests that eating vegetables and fruits pertinent to the season has better nutritional benefits."

"Why this discussion today? Any particular reason? Is today a day of vegetables or something?" asked Keith.

"Thank you. Master Keith. Every day must be the day of vegetables and fruits. Our food habits in India have undergone a sea change in the last 50 years. Unfortunately, not all the changes are healthy. So, we must remember that plant-based diets and cuisine rich in greens, locally available vegetables, and fruits can reduce health issues and contribute to an environmentally sustainable solution. I have made it my mandate to explain this to the younger generation. That said, I will no longer stand between the delicious entree and you. Thank you!"

Chef Virupaksha bowed.

All of them clapped.

"Bravo Chef. Best lecture I ever heard."

"Super. It's a great topic."

"Thank you, Virupaksha. I wanted our younger generation to understand your deep passion for Indian culinary traditions. I hope they will now appreciate Indian food better than before," said Queen Mother appreciatively.

Food was served on a large silver plate with a green banana leaf. Pulihora or spiced tamarind rice, mamidikaya pappu (raw mango dal), panasapottu koora (jackfruit curry), kanda-bachali koora (yam and basella curry), gutti vankaya koora (tender brinjals in a spicy gravy), ulava charu (thick, horse gram lentil soup), dosa avakaya (yellow cucumber pickle), kandi podi, (powder of roasted toor dal and spices), were served with steaming hot rice, fresh butter, and aromatic ghee. Crispy vodiyalu and appadalu (papad) were served as side dishes. Boorelu (a sweetmeat made with jaggery and urad dal), jalebis, pala kova (dried and sweetened whole milk), and pootharekulu (a paper-thin dessert made from rice starch, jaggery, and clarified butter) were the desserts. All were typical of a Telugu household.

They all ate in silence.

Finally, after everything was cleared, mint ice cream was served to 'cleanse the palette.' That was not all. A large silver compote was brought around, on which lay an array of miniature sweets: fresh strawberries, tiny eclairs, mini chum chums (traditional Bengali sweet), and fresh fruit salad.

"Hmm, too delicious, Chef."

"Simply too scrumptious!"

"God, I can hardly breathe. I overate!"

Queen Mother smiled discreetly at all their *oohs-aahs* since all of them did manage to put away substantial quantities of food.

"Thank you, Chef, it was the most wonderful vegetarian meal I ever had. I am so amazed at the number of courses you prepare in India. It was a very enlightening evening today," thanked Keith formally.

"Does this mean you will lay off palak paneer?" teased Janice.

"Never! It will be my all-time favorite," laughed Keith.

As they were talking, Durga suddenly noticed someone come through the door. It was her father!

"Where is Lakshmi?" asked Dr. Varma blankly.

"Nanna? Nanna?" Durga rushed to her father's side. But his face had gone blank again. Queen Mother went to him and held his hand. He nodded. Two nurses in uniform gently escorted him back to his room.

Durga's face dimmed. Her grandmother came to her and held her hand. Durga held back her tears.

For the first time, he remembered her mother's name! Clearly, the herb was showing some results! But it wasn't enough.

They all went back to their rooms. Durga flipped open her photo gallery. She kept browsing all the happy pics with her dad and mom. Suddenly, the picture she had taken of the parchment popped up. She studied it for some time.

Why was there a quote about Soma and poison in the parchment? Did it lead to someplace with plant-based poisons? The Book of Poisons did mention Kings used poisons. So, was there a connection with her family?

Durga opened her father's journal again. Two of the pages seemed stuck to each other. As she pried them open carefully, a blank parchment paper fell out! Durga put it on the table, rolled on to her bed and fell asleep.

Chapter Twelve

Adrian Picks up the Scent

The sun was setting.

It was nearly March. Snow was still abundant. Adrian sat near the porch, which had a beautiful view of the Rhine River in Germany.

Adrian's house was also his office. It was a typical traditional, timbered German house from pre-war times with an A-frame roof, so particular to the Bavarian style. A small front porch oversaw a large oak tree. At the back was a large garden filled with a fascinating variety of plants. The interiors were done up entirely in wood with loft-like levels and large windows to let in the sun. There was an extended part of the house which functioned as his office. There was a large meeting hall and another spacious floor space with workstations. The place was state-of-the-art. It just didn't look like that from the outside. No one would give it a second glance. Adrian preferred it that way. He never drove a fancy car, and never wore expensive suits. His everyday wear included a neatly washed pair of jeans teamed with rugged cowboy boots and fresh white or light blue shirts.

Adrian looked around with a sense of pride. His heart

always swelled up when he saw his home. He turned around as he heard a car drive up. A nondescript wagon loaded with firewood parked just beyond the porch. Two thickset men got down carrying a small package.

Adrian's heart skipped a beat. He had been waiting for this moment for a long time!

He walked casually to his office, and the men followed him. Once inside, he anxiously collected the pouch that the men held up. It was no ordinary pouch. Concealed cleverly, it was temperature-controlled and with conditions of a hot spring inside.

Adrian's eyes lit up as he saw what was inside.

"Nymphaea thermarum, the smallest water lily plant in the world," breathed Adrian.

Almost extinct, the plant was carefully nurtured to life by Spanish scientific horticulturist Carlos Magdalena, who re-created the hot spring conditions by heating mud in London's Botanical Gardens.

This was the last one of its kind in the world!

"Was there any trouble?"

"None at all, Adrian. It was a clean-cut job. After three weeks, Crime Units closed the case. Plant theft is not their priority anyways. But we waited till the time was right to get it to you."

"Good. Good. That is the way a job is to be done. Well, here is your payment,"

Adrian handed over a brown paper bag that had two large wads amounting to nearly $50,000! The two men pocketed the bag, and left.

Adrian turned around to look at the lovely lotus. "I was waiting for you for a long, long time," he murmured as he circled, admiring its beauty.

This would fetch him at least five million dollars from the Japanese collector. *It's worth all the trouble!*

Adrian Gerber's love for Botany and identifying plants had led him to become an expert in Plant Genetics and Entomology.

Adrian returned to the porch and stood admiring the view.

He saw his best friend and associate, Van den Bosch, walking towards him.

Van den Bosch was in many ways quite different than him. Born in the Netherlands, 'Bosch' as he has always been called — was an atypical Dutchman but educated in Germany. Loud, flashy, but brilliant, Bosch liked 'unearthing' rare orchids and identifying them for Governments. When he met Adrian, he was working for Dr. Scale, a noted botanist who had founded a company that identified rare species. Adrian too decided to work for Dr. Scale's company.

Over the next few years, Adrian and Bosch went on

several missions to Peru and Thailand to 'uncover' the rarest of rare flora, fauna and document them. As they worked worldwide, they stumbled into the world of 'plant heist,' which was both lucrative and easy.

Poaching plants from various locations from either badly guarded national gardens or open places like cliffs was easier than they had anticipated. They found that there was a thriving black market for these. Finally, they started their own company called 'Seltenheit GmbH, which 'sourced' rare plants for enthusiastic gardeners. Also, some very rare ones for 'secret' collectors.

Back to the present...Bosch approached Adrian quietly.

"I have no reports after Pushpa got killed. I'm not too fond of Krishna Murthy, who has Dr. Uwe's mobile phone. He says there is nothing to report. I think he's cleverer than he looks, and he's probably playing us."

"Patience, my friend. *Kleinvieh macht auch Mist* (Even small things, or small amounts, can still contribute to a larger result). For the time being, we need to back off. Well, there is nothing to connect us with Krishna Murthy. We made sure of that. So, the gadget in Pushpa's room will now give away nothing. Meanwhile, keep a close eye on the house."

Bosch nodded. He blindly trusted Adrian's instincts.

Adrian stepped into his massive, well-organized library. It was his favorite sanctuary.

He took up the file of Dr. Harish Varma and started reading again.

Adrian was in awe of Dr. Varma. He kept his life simple despite having everything: wealth, position, a loving family, and great recognition. He pursued his hunt for rare germplasm in the most disciplined and organized manner. It was the most unselfish thing to do because his country's Government seemed oblivious to its importance. Dr. Varma often struggled to get his voice heard.

Adrian admired that trait. He constantly compared himself with Dr. Varma. Though Adrian knew his hunt was for selfish reasons, he hoped he could become legitimate one day after he had made enough money.

He sighed and looked at a photograph of Dr. Varma with his family. His eyes lingered on Durga a few moments more. A scornful expression came into his eyes.

From all the reports he had heard so far about her, she was anything but impressive. There was no sign of her father's prowess visible in her. Durga was shy, clingy, introverted, and had no talent for botany — she even failed simple quiz competitions! Adrian had won awards, scholarships, and great recognition at the same age. He had no patience for the lazy ones.

His thoughts returned to Dr. Varma. And his quest.

Adrian had been tracking Dr. Varma for years. It was the easiest thing to do. His formula was rather simple. Once Dr. Varma rediscovered a rare plant, Adrian waited for a few months and promptly stole it. There had been so many examples. Dr. Varma seemed to know this and had started to take precautions, but Adrian was always getting the better of him. The last couple of years, however, had been different. Ever since his coronation, there was a slight change in Dr. Varma's search pattern. He seemed to be searching for something very particular.

What plant variety? Rare for sure, why the utter secrecy? This, Adrian could not fathom. He had planted a super-talented spy, Pushpa, at the Devdi. But even she could feed him very small morsels of information. Adrian started suspecting her loyalty. To keep an eye on her, he managed to have his associates contact Krishna Murthy, the estate manager. Adrian was aware that he had a criminal record and was doing some spying for Dhyaneshwara Raju. Adrian's associates quickly recruited him, giving him bribes. But there was constant friction between him and Pushpa. Adrian had been listening to these complaints and wanted to speak to Pushpa, but she had died before he could do so. According to Krishna Murthy, it was an accident. But Adrian had his own doubts.

In retrospect, I should have foreseen it, Adrian winced. He didn't like to be wrong.

Adrian walked to the elegantly carved wooden bureau and poured himself a white Reisling wine from a delicate decanter. Absently, he gazed at an impressionist painting that hung on one of the walls. It was a rare work — Le Jardin de Mirbeau aux Damps, Octave Mirbeau's garden in Damps, 1891 by Camille Pissarro, a Danish-French Impressionist. Adrian acquired it as an anonymous collector at one of those fancy auctions in Paris. He felt he could relate to Pissarro much more than the other Impressionists of his time. Even though Pissarro played a vital role in the furtherance of the Impressionist movement, he was also a bit of an underdog. Adrian liked underdogs and their 'struggle.'

Just then, Bosch stepped into the library.

"Adrian, someone has been hacking into our databases. Our technical team has detected a minor breach. Of course, we have ramped up our firewalls. Nothing seems out of place," said Bosch casually.

Adrian frowned.

"Track that breach. It might be important."

"But Adrian, it was only a minor one. Some freak may have..."

"Just do it!"

"Ok. Meanwhile, I investigated Pushpa's device to find one unsent message. But it has to be switched on. I will send a message to KM. I think it may lead us to something important! Also, on instinct, I hacked into Dr. Harish's WhatsApp records and found two interesting words - poison, weapon — in his texts to Dr. Kennedy Chandrasekhar. Looks like we have hit the jackpot!" The excitement in Bosch's voice was palpable.

Adrian's heart raced. But outwardly, he maintained his calm.

"Bosch, this is fantastic news," replied Adrian matter-of-factly.

"One more thing: Durga's handmaid was seen prowling near Pushpa's room."

Well. Well Well. Was KM up to something? No. Suma had virtually no connection to KM. Only to Durga. Did Durga enter the scene? She may be up to something. But what? wondered Adrian.

"Okay. Track Durga. Keep an eye on Krishna Murthy as well. Access Pushpa's device and check if there is something there."

"Yes, Adrian. Will do."

Bosch looked surprised; Adrian was almost talking to himself. But, it was not his place to question Adrian's commands. He merely nodded, pushing his hands inside his soft leather jacket, and stepped away.

Adrian's mind was racing. *Poison? Poison plants? Weapon?*

Suddenly he sat up, his heart racing.

So, that was it. The heirloom must be about a weapon that was connected to plants. This was not unusual. Throughout history, plant poison has been used in weaponry. It was certainly very advanced in India. Mahabharata had references to many powerful and unusual weapons. Dr. Varma may have inherited something exceptional — the access to which will give the owner great power!

Chapter Thirteen

An Unusual Clue, An Unusual Treasure

Durga was alone. Janice had gone off for a walk. Abhik and Keith were busy with their pending school assignments.

She walked over to the flask, boiled some water, and made herself a green tea with a spot of honey, cinnamon, and tulasi leaves.

She set the steaming cup near the journal and checked her messages when she realized that words and pictures started mysteriously appearing on the blank parchment that had fallen out of her father's journal!

She screamed, almost knocking off the cup. For a moment, she stared at the page, terrified. Slowly, she willed her mind to focus on the page.

There were very fine illustrations of different plants, and underneath each was a line in Sanskrit. Stuffing the journal in her bag, she ran out of the room, texting all her friends to join her. All of them assembled within minutes.

"Guys, look at this. Till about 30 minutes ago, this parchment was blank, and suddenly, when I looked, these words had appeared mysteriously. It was practically spooky!"

"D, take a breath and relax. What were you doing while reading the journal?" asked Abhik calmly.

"Nothing, I mean, I made myself some green tea and..."

"Aha, it is crystal clear to me!" exclaimed Abhik.

"What, Abhi?"

"Invisible ink! You know the ancients always used this. Quite a common practice. Goes back 5000 years. In India, it was a well-established practice. Exposure to heat reveals the hidden words. So what's in it?"

"Some illustrations and lines in Sanskrit. There are also additional lines below. Here Keith. Please tell me what it means?"

"Let's magnify the image in my Android magnifying Glass app," suggested Abhik.

Keith pored over the magnified image for a few minutes, making a lot of notes.

"Well, the line under each plant describes the plant. Wait a minute, aren't these plants poisonous??" stopped Keith in mid-sentence.

"Yes, these are some of the most poisonous plants in the world!" said Durga, studying the illustrations.

"Yes, I have 'The Book of Poisons in India' by Uncle Kenny. The book says there are over 4000 species of medicinal plants growing as shrubs, herbs, and trees in India, many of which are poisonous when administered in large doses. Look, this is Cleistanthus collinus — all its parts are very toxic, and its poison has no antidote! Then this looks like it is Antiaris toxicaria; of course, there are several species of the same. This one may have existed then! In any case, its latex contains a highly toxic cardiac glycoside that can result in a massive heart attack within seconds; in tropical Asia, it is the perfect source of poison for arrows and darts!" said Durga hurriedly, as she thumbed through the book.

Janice and Abhik became very quiet. Keith continued to study the verses.

"Wait a minute, here are some recipes...my God!!! D. Are you thinking what I am thinking?"

"Yes, Keith, I think so. I think these recipes are to kill! What's more...plant poisons cannot be traced after a short while of ingestion. So the culprit will go scot free!" concluded Durga.

"Is it some freakish aberration, guys?" asked Janice.

"On the contrary, a very well-thought-out war strategy. Remember, Chanakya advised his king to use it as a weapon. Phytochemicals as bioweapons! What a brilliant idea!" exclaimed Abhik.

"That means the one who discovers it will have immense power!" breathed Keith.

"Exactly! It will have devastating consequences in the wrong hands!" said Durga, dropping her voice to a whisper.

"Hey guys, look, there is another verse in chaste Sanskrit right at the bottom, in fine print. And a small motif here. Here it goes. The verse says that a treasure lies at the base of a Shiva temple surrounded by the sea. This treasure will sustain the Earth. The custodians of this treasure are the Gajendrapatirajus. Only a true regal heir can unravel this treasure. But for that he or she has to solve a series of clues. On gaining access, he/she needs to nurture it until it is passed on to another worthy successor," said Keith, translating the lines.

"So, my dad must have started unraveling the clues but was midway. Just so nobody could get their hands on these, he may have used invisible ink."

"Yes, D," agreed Abhik.

"Do you think the treasure is this poison stuff? If so, it's very disappointing; treasures are supposed to be interesting, like-like..." Janice was babbling away as usual.

"Jenny, can you please be quiet for a few moments? Now the map adds up. Look!" she showed them the image, telling them how she had found it in her regal sword.

"Aha, so this is your quest, D!" exclaimed Abhik.

"It is actually a quest for poison. Wonder why they call it a treasure?" quipped Janice.

"This needs work. God, we need to refer journals and..and.." Durga's excitement was palpable.

"Yes, but we have the Interschool Quiz and the Spring Ball coming up next week," reminded Janice.

"Oh, that torture! Torture!" said Durga glumly

"Yes, I wonder if we can avoid it?" wondered Keith.

"No, Principal ma'am already warned us —no one can miss it!"

Durga nodded sadly.

Monday dawned bright, and they were back at school.

The following day, Durga, Janice, Keith, and Abhik were summoned by Professor Jaywant. They saw her poring over a journal as usual. A sense of respect crept into Durga's heart. *She was always trying her best.*

"Well, I heard some good feedback from the old age home and the beach activity. I am happy that you took the detention in the right spirit and gave your best. I hereby relieve you from the same."

"Thank you, Ma'am. But we don't want to be relieved," said Durga

Professor Jaywant was taken aback.

"Yes, Ma'am. These two months have been the best time

of our lives. We learned a lot and focused our energies on a good cause. We would like your support in continuing it," said Durga earnestly.

Professor Jaywant smiled.

"Of course, I will speak with Madam Roy and arrange special days for you to continue your good work in the old age home and also the beach cleaning effort."

Akanksha, Jagannath, and Elizabeth walked in. Both groups glared at each other and left.

Just as they crossed the room, Janice shushed them. They huddled behind some desks and listened in.

"Well, Akanksha, Jagannath, and Elizabeth, I now relieve you of the detention; however, I have heard some unfavorable reports about using some unwarranted medication without proper medical support or advice. Let me tell you, it is downright dangerous! You will lose some points for the same."

"Bu-but, Ma'am, Durga and her friends have..." argued Akanksha angrily.

"Akanksha, please don't argue. It's a different case with Durga. She is well-versed in traditional medicine, having learned the same from her dad, a great researcher. It comes naturally to her. Every time, she has proven herself by using her skills to save a life or solve a problem using very basic medicinal herbs known even to my grandmother. Only we have forgotten the use of them."

Durga felt surprised and happy at how the professor interpreted her actions. *It all feels good!*

Janice, Keith, and Abhik gave her a fist bump silently.

"Bu-but this is outrageous, Professor!!" Akanksha was practically yelling

"To your credit, you did something good too! I am not turning a blind eye to everything!"

Akanksha stopped to listen.

"You, Jagannath, and Elizabeth have spruced up the place, making it cleaner and nicer looking with pretty illustrations for kids. That initiative to collect old toys and books was also a nice gesture. For that, I will grant you some additional points. Now, off you all go. I have work to do."

Akanksha's face swelled with pride. Jagannath and Elizabeth smiled, too.

"Thank you, Ma'am!" they chorused, and left.

"Come guys, we will make some good PR out of this. I will tell my dad to arrange for some press articles."

The feel-good factor of completing the detention was quickly forgotten as the final date of the Interschool Quiz competitions drew near, which was being hosted by Magnolia. Durga, Janice, Keith, and Abhik decided to participate as a team, with Durga as the team-lead. The minute they registered, Akanksha, Jagannath, and Elizabeth gave in their names.

The next big topic was the Magnolia Evening Spring Ball.

There were so many things to be done. Whenever Akanksha's team ran across Durga's team, they smirked with a superior air, promptly infuriating Janice.

"Look at their faces! Stupid louts…why those superior smiles? Diggy, you are wearing us down, buddy. How many more weeks of this practice madness?" complained Janice even as Durga drove her team to practice as someone possessed. This was the first time they saw Durga like this!

Twenty schools from across the country had sent in participating teams. Well over 100 students accompanied by their professors came in two days before the event.

The hot lunch topic was the Evening Spring Ball and what to wear. The management of Magnolia had given out fliers with elaborate rules such as — 'Ladies' outfits need to be of tea length (mid-calf) and one piece — a dress, not a skirt and blouse. No mid-riff baring or see-through dresses. No strapless gowns; Boys must be dressed in 'Dark suits, white-winged collars, and formal shoes.'

Every year, Professor Kate Williams, the Head of the English Department, oversaw the Evening Spring Ball. Music was always a blend of new and retro-western pop.

In fact, in their zeal to practice for the Quiz, Durga and

Janice had forgotten entirely about their dresses.

As the final day drew near, a festive spirit prevailed, and the school was transformed; the garden looked spectacular, the library was given a thorough dusting, even the brass knobs on the lab doors glinted.

The Interstate Quiz was set in the much-lauded Aurora auditorium. The circular, dome-like structure, with glass-curtained walls on all sides, a large atrium on the top, and wooden flooring, offered a complete view of the school grounds.

The evening before the big day, Durga received a call from her grandmother. After half an hour of giving her an entire lowdown on the events at school, Durga felt deeply relieved. Her father was better. She thought *Bamma is a real stress-buster* as she walked towards her room. Opening the door, she found four large packages waiting on the bed.

As she walked towards them, Janice burst into the room, as usual, in a dramatic fashion. "Diggy, you will never know what that Akanksha girl is planning! She…wow, Diggy, what are these?" she stopped mid-sentence and exclaimed. The packages bore each of their names. They eagerly ripped off the neat packaging to find two very elegant evening gowns: pale pink for Janice and periwinkle blue for Durga. The gently appliquéd gowns were very classy. Of exactly tea-length, they fitted the girls perfectly. There were shoes and accessories to match. There were two well-tailored suits for Abhik and Keith!

Hope you have a great time, dears! said a small note bearing the royal insignia of the Gajendrapatirajus. "Bamma, thank you, thank you!" yelled Janice as she broke into a mad little dance with Durga. They both burst out laughing and flopped on to the bed.

The day dawned bright. As Durga smelled the air outside the window, she felt an unusual calm. She knew the day was going to turn out in her favor. *Just pure instinct*, she thought happily as Janice stirred in her bed, wanting to catch that last bit of sleep before the alarms went off.

Calmly, Durga, Janice, Keith, and Abhik arrived early, finding their seats in the Aurora Auditorium. The organization was meticulous. The hall was packed. The participating teams were already seated.

At 9:00 AM, Principal Roy stepped on the stage, looking very distinguished in a cream, silk handwoven Bhagalpur saree.

"Dear participants, a warm welcome to you all from Magnolia. It gives me great pleasure to see you all here. I request Mr. Pratik Jain, the Quiz Master, to take over the proceedings. May the best team win!"

A round of applause went around the room. Pratik waved cheerily as he walked to the dais. He cleared his throat, and started speaking.

"Well, let's get to the game, eh? We have 12 participating teams today. There will be a total of 50 questions split into five rounds of 10 questions each. There would be standard rounds, table rounds (you need to mark in the sheets given to you), and wipe-out rounds. Please remember that the wipe-out rounds are very stringent. No wrong answers or 'guessing' the answers since if you put a wrong answer, you get a negative marking which means you can lose points. For the Twitterati, please note that the hashtags are #Biodiversityquiz and #pratik jain, along with your usual ones," paused Pratik as he looked in Professor Anantanarayan's direction for confirmation. She nodded with a smile.

"Finally, in the possibility of a tie-breaker situation where two or more teams finish with the same score overall, there will be a 'lightning' question. The team that answers this correctly will win the Quiz. Let's begin!"

As the names of the participating teams and their respective schools were announced, the crowd cheered, especially for the Magnolia teams with Durga's Team and Akanksha's team.

The Quiz competition began. Both the teams did well in the initial rounds. After a disastrous wipe-out round, Akanksha and the team were out. Durga and the team held on by a thin thread to reach the finals.

"Ah-ha...so what do we have here? A perfect time to have a tie-breaker! All right, this will be an interesting one," exclaimed Pratik, rubbing his hands in glee.

Durga and her team looked at each other anxiously.

"Here it is. The clincher," bellowed Pratik as he signaled to his team. They wheeled in a package-like thing covered with silver foil on a small trolley.

Pratik pulled off the foil with a flourish and looked around triumphantly. It was a large potted plant.

Loud 'oohs' went up in the room.

"I believe, and I hope you all agree, that the topic of biodiversity doesn't exist in books but out there… starts with our garden. How many of us can identify plants in our backyard?"

Pratik looked around the hall. Confused faces glowered back at him.

"Magnolia and Good Shepherd. Here's your tie-breaker question. Identify this plant. One of your team members can come closer and have a look."

Complete silence ensued. No one spoke or stirred. The team from Good Shepherd looked dazed. After hectic consultations, the team announced,

"We will pass this question."

"Magnolia, it's your turn."

Durga's heart leapt with happiness. Without a second's hesitation, she pressed the buzzer.

"Murraya paniculata, commonly called orange jasmine or orange jessamine, china box or mock orange. It is a species of shrub or small tree in the family Rutaceae and is native to South Asia, Southeast Asia, and Australia."

A great silence fell across the room.

"Don't you want to come closer and examine the plant?"

"No," said Durga confidently.

"Correct answer," roared Pratik Jain, and the hall exploded.

Durga and team had brought home the prestigious Interschool Quiz Trophy to Magnolia!

Chapter Fourteen

A Victory, Finally!

"Excellent, Magnolia! You have done it. Brilliant! Dear participants, I hope you liked being a part of this Quiz. As I always say, quizzing opens your mind to new things and experiences. The teams here today did an excellent job. Thank you for allowing me to be your quiz master. *Ciao*." Pratik Jain stepped down to a deafening applause.

A happy blur ensued; the elated students lifted Durga and her team members onto their shoulders.

After the Quiz, it was time to prepare for the Evening Spring Ball. The event was to start at 7:00 PM, and there were a few hours left still. Durga and Janice decided to take a quick nap. They hadn't slept in days. They fell asleep the minute they hit the bed.

The loud trilling of their mobile phones woke them up. Durga and Janice looked at each other. "Wha...," a still groggy Janice was about to get up even as Durga sprinted up to reach the mobiles.

“What are you doing, sleepy-heads? In one hour, we have to report for the Ball. When are you all coming?” demanded Keith

“Give us half an hour, and we will be there…” muttered Durga.

One hour later, they were all assembled near the Basketball court to see it completely transformed into a charming party scene being the venue for the Evening Spring Ball.

The evening was perfect. A light breeze ruffled off the top of the trees. The sky had turned purple, now replete with a crescent moon and shining stars.

In the excitement of the Quiz and preparing for the evening, Durga had not thought of what lay before her. And now, she felt a sense of growing exhilaration. For the first time in many days, she felt nicely dressed. This gave her confidence. Abhik, Keith looked pretty smart in their jackets.

As she caught sight of herself in the looking glass near the entrance, she couldn’t distinguish herself from the rest; a procession of young ladies in white, blue, and pink dresses, boys in formal bow-ties mingled into one radiant congregation in the light and brilliance of the setting. As they entered together, a cheer went through the already-settled crowd. The regular hum of voices, footsteps, and greetings nearly deafened Durga.

Even the teachers have made an attempt to blend in,

thought Durga on seeing them all in elegant gowns.

A sudden commotion at the entrance made everyone turn around. As the crowds moved aside, Akanksha stepped forward, looking like a vision, in a stylish Dior gown. Jagannath Mishra, Elizabeth Waltham, who had also dressed elegantly for a change, came forward from behind her and stood next to her. For one brief moment, Durga felt a loss she couldn't explain.

It's perfect! And chic.

Akanksha's eyes shone as she caught sight of Durga's 'look,' and she flashed her superior smile. Durga and her friends nodded a curt 'hello' and mingled with the rest.

By 7:00 PM, everyone had assembled. A bell tinkled somewhere.

Principal Roy came onto the stage. A roar of enthusiastic claps greeted her. She smiled as she took up the microphone to present her opening remarks.

"Dear Students, I am delighted once again to extend a warm welcome to all of you to the Magnolia Evening Spring Ball. Several interesting programs will be presented here today. The décor is splendid. All the House Teams have contributed well. I feel it's time to announce that 50 points are awarded to all the House Teams: APJ Abdul Kalam, MS Swaminathan, CV Raman and Mokshagundam Visveswarayya. I am delighted to award an extra 50 points to APJ Abdul Kalam House and heartily congratulate Durga

Varma and her team mates, Janice Chandrasekhar, Keith Myers, and Abhik Bannerjee, for winning the prestigious Interstate Quiz Competition so effortlessly."

As the spotlight focused on the triumphant four, the whole crowd cheered for one full minute.

Principal Roy resumed her speech.

"Recently, Professor Jaywant shared an interesting fact. Two teams were given detention to do social work, but what they did with it turned out to be a great contribution, setting an excellent example. I would like Durga Varma to come up here and say a few words, followed by Akanksha Raju."

Janice pressed Durga's hand. Abhik and Keith smiled at Durga, who felt very light-headed. She walked up to the stage as though in a dream.

Durga went up and looked at the crowd. She could hear her heart pounding. Only, this time, she felt an unusual calm.

Janice held her breath, Keith shuffled restlessly, and Abhik held the mobile to capture it all on video.

"Good evening all, I am honored to stand here, but the victory belongs to all of Magnolia."

Thunderous applause greeted Durga.

"My friends Janice, Keith, Abhik, and I visited an old age home as a part of our detention. We quickly realized that with some planning, we could make a real change. Thank you all for contributing to the crowdfunding we organized, for every penny counted in our efforts to provide the inmates a better way of life. The Vodarevu beach cleaning activity was exciting, too.

My mom quotes from a book she likes very much - The Alchemist by Paulo Coelho — *When you want something, all the universe conspires in helping you to achieve it.* My team and I realized for the first time that if we do good things, there are people who will walk with us. Support us. We have decided to continue the effort. Please do join with us... yes?"

"Yes!" roared Magnolia.

Durga smiled.

"Thank you! Namaskarams to my teachers, parents, grandmother, and best wishes to all my friends. Enjoy the evening."

Deafening applause made Durga dizzy. Janice, Keith, and Abhik hugged her as she came down the aisle.

Janice had tears in her eyes. "You are exceptional, Diggy, you know! How well you spoke!"

"How many times have you said we instead of I, D. You are terrific," complimented Abhik in his quiet way.

"Proud to be your friend," Keith shook hands with Durga.

Many students rushed towards her, asking for selfies.

It was Akanksha's turn to speak.

"Well, as a leader, I can do quite a lot. All those children were downtrodden. I wanted to help them. I went all out. I spent a lot of my personal money as well, which was my pocket money. I got so much appreciation from everywhere for it. You know, even the press wrote about it. Because of me, our school came into the spotlight."

A thin ripple of claps greeted Akanksha as she stepped away. Elizabeth and Jagannath looked deflated, utterly ignored by Akanksha in her speech.

The cultural programs began, and everybody had a great time.

The dinner was laid out as a buffet with many courses. The dessert counter with its delicious array was the most crowded!

As Durga and her friends sat down to have their dinner, Akanksha and her friends appeared from nowhere.

"How is the Ball going, Princess? Disappointing? It turns out you and your friends are nothing but boring geeks. Look at the following we have on social media— 5000 likes and counting," sneered Akanksha.

"Seriously, Akku?? Didn't you see??" Janice's anger was mounting by the second. Durga laid a calming hand on Janice and spoke up.

"You are nothing but a bully, and yes, certainly a smartly dressed one, I will give you that. I notice you didn't even thank your best friends for all their contributions."

Akanksha turned around to look at Elizabeth and Jagannath, who looked positively belligerent, and laughed.

"They?.. It wasn't necessary. After all, I am the leader, and they follow me!"

"Akku, tell you what? I have the most incredible friends on Earth. We don't need social media likes to prove people LIKE us. We have REAL people in the REAL world willing to help us. I like this a lot better! Peace out!" countered Durga.

"Oh, is it? All the meek and the ugly say the same thing!"

"*Hear. Hear. O, beware, my lord, of jealousy;*

It is the green-eyed monster which doth mock

The meat it feeds on," quoted Keith.

"Oh wow! Shakespeare, Othello, well done!" applauded Elizabeth Waltham enthusiastically.

"Oh shut up, Lizzy!" shouted Akanksha as she stormed out.

The ball was followed by a few days of holidays.

Durga and friends were back at the Devdi, lounging, and binge-watching a few seasons of a mystery series. Abhik had his laptop open.

Suddenly, Abhik gave a start. Keith paused the video and

looked questioningly at Abhik.

"KM is up to something funny. I have been carefully monitoring the camera feed these last few weeks without surprises. Now, he's near Pushpa's cottage. I will project it on my laptop. Come, have a look."

Durga, Janice, and Keith gathered around.

Krishna Murthy was indeed acting surreptitiously.

He went straight down to Pushpa's cottage, glanced around, and let himself in.

"Aha, he has switched on Pushpa's device. Tracking, tracking, yes. I can see a message. Going...going to a server in Germany. Oh, what's the message? Gotcha — I captured it! Ha, there-oh, switched off? And...gone!"

All of them sat stunned for a few moments.

"Well, what did Pushpa's device transmit?" asked Durga slowly.

"D, don't blow your top..."

"Okay, Abhi, I won't," Durga's voice was tight with apprehension.

"It's the parchment from the sword. By switching on the device, he has transmitted the picture. It was probably lying in the outbox."

"Wh-what?" screamed Durga.

Janice and Keith did their best to hold Durga and calm her down.

"D, give me a few minutes. I am tracking the servers. It went to Adrian Gerber," finished Abhik.

"Oh my God! The so-called treasure might as well be a weapon in the wrong hands! We must do something to prevent those guys from ever finding it! But how do we do it?" muttered Durga pacing up and down.

A bell tinkled, and they all jumped to see Suma carrying a sealed envelope.

"Durgamma, you have a letter."

Durga gingerly opened the envelope, and her face went white. Janice, Keith, and Abhik rushed to her.

"Diggy, what is it?"

"I-I received a letter...from my father."

"How come? Diggy? He's right here! And his memory —" Janice stopped abruptly.

"Maybe he sent this before. I wonder if he knew he would be attacked?" Durga was speaking almost to herself.

"What? How?" murmured Janice, utterly confused.

"Well, any clues as to where it was posted from?" asked Keith.

"It was supposed to be hand delivered, maybe," said

Durga, looking at the Royal Seal.

"Well, what is in it?"

A frazzled Durga began to talk a bit abruptly, "A twig and a letter…."

"A twig? What twig?" demanded Abhik.

"It's a dried twig with light violet plum-colored flower blossoms. It looks very unusual."

"WHAT?" Keith almost shouted

"Shut up… don't shout, for heaven's sake! I am trying to think."

"Right-o, sorry! Go on, D," murmured Abhik.

Nanna's message is most definitely a shock! Maybe it ought to have come sooner?

"What's in the letter?" repeated Janice, unable to restrain her curiosity.

"Let me read it," said Durga as she read it aloud.

Dearest…

The last few days have been fascinating. The landscape here is enchanting. I will bring you and your mother with me here the next time. There is so much to know still. Nature is a great teacher.

I have only touched the shore of a vast ocean. I am climbing a mountain to understand new things. It's a temple of knowledge. One must have a fierce determination to conquer knowledge. I sometimes think of our family deity Nrusimha – that fierceness in resolution, that sword of defiance…is what precisely must show us the right path…

Once you understand this, there is only one purpose. To protect this knowledge from the prying eyes of evil and nurture it for future generations. That must be our goal in life. There is so much I need to tell you. Sometimes in life, there seems to be so little time! One must have courage.

I shall see you soon. My resolution this year is to …

"It's incomplete. Moreover, there's nothing here. Just a description of the trip and some gyan. But the twig, it must mean something."

"Oh, for heaven's sake, Diggy, what is this business with the twig?" said Keith worriedly

"Well, Dad would always leave me a riddle by way of dried leaves or flowers. I had to identify the plant, which usually means something."

She found a pen and scribbled down all the clues to identify the plant.

"No way," she got up.

"What Diggy?" asked Janice

"This plant is unique! Let me see if my father's journal has any clues. Nothing here."

Durga frowned. *Could it be a new species?* she wondered.

"Abhik, just Google all the new plant species found in the last year."

"That's way too much scope, D!"

"Well, how about the twin states of Andhra Pradesh and Telangana?"

"Done and done. Hey, D, here, have a look."

Durga scanned all the links.

"Here, Emilia reddyi."

"What is that?" asked all of them together.

"Oh yes. The plant is named after my father's friend Dr. Reddy, the Taxonomist! I remember him mentioning it to me. Here is the news report. Two researchers have found a new plant species on the Galikonda Hill in the Araku Valley tribal area of Visakhapatnam district. The researchers attribute the species to the Asteraceae family — a plant with light violet plum-colored flowers that blossoms between September and February. The researchers have grouped it under the 'critically endangered' category."

"So, what does this mean?" implored Abhik.

Durga went utterly quiet.

"Guys, everything makes sense now. This species is from Araku Valley. Where was my father working before the accident? Araku Valley. He mentions an ocean. The timing of this blossom matches with my dad being there! Let's look at the scroll from the sword. Aren't we looking for something at the top of the mountain? Could it be that there is a temple in the vicinity? The clue in this twig is that it is 'endangered' — which means whatever is there in Araku Valley in that temple, if it exists, is rare and highly..."

"Poisonous! Bingo, Diggy, that's a lot of information to process. You are a genius!"

Eureka. Eureka. Squawked Nibbles.

Janice hugged Durga. Keith and Abhik high-fived noisily.

"Now it seems fairly clear. We need to look for a temple atop the mountain in Araku Valley. Is there one?" wondered Durga.

"This is a really strong clue. Let's explore it." said Abhik.

Chapter Fifteen

Tapping the Clues in Germany

"Well, not before our Germany trip! We also need to prepare," said Janice warningly.

"Oh no! I almost forgot. What are our dates?" groaned Durga.

"We have just two weeks from today," said Janice.

"Hey, I remembered something. That Adrian Gerber. Doesn't he stay somewhere near Cologne?" exclaimed Keith.

"You are absolutely brill, Keith! So true. Maybe we could sneak out and find some clues," chirped Durga happily.

"Guys, is anyone hungry?" asked Janice

"You betcha," yelled all of them together.

The topic of discussion shifted to Germany almost immediately.

"We need to complete our shopping for the Germany trip. accuweather.com shows the night temperatures as below -2° C, brrr! We must make sure to pack some warm clothes,"

Charismatic plant thief plots...

Keith was already lecturing away.

"Ah, the German expert is speaking..." laughed Janice.

Durga turned towards the window. She remembered her grandmother's advice as she watched the bright blue sky. *Just focus on the one thing that is crucial at the moment. The answers for the rest would come in eventually.*

They landed in Cologne, to 3° C temperature, snow and rain. Professor Jaywant and Professor Anantanarayan had traveled with them. Though they were all well wrapped in warm clothes, the chill came through. They huddled close to each other for warmth as their taxi took them through the streets of Cologne. They cheered as they passed the Wilhemplatz – a popular food market with rows of colourful stalls overflowing with fresh fruit, bread, cheese, and vegetables. It was packed with locals pouring in from the nearby Florastrasse U-Bahn subway, stopping their trolleys to stock up for the week. The flower seller in the northwest corner presented a delightful sight, crammed with tall stalks of cream-pink roses, gerberas, chrysanthemums, and daisies.

They could briefly glimpse the twin spires of the famous Dom Cathedral and the sparkling Rhine River from the street. They sighed in relief as they entered the warm and cozy common room at St. George's, The Global School. The school was bustling with students who had arrived from various parts of the world, to participate in the Quiz. The day passed quickly with registrations, getting the passes, and checking into the dorm rooms, which were quite comfortably furnished.

It was -2° C the following day. Durga woke up with a start as her alarm went off at 6:30 AM local time. Even her bones felt chilled. They had to report at 8:00 AM. She snuggled into her blanket for another 10 minutes before she willed herself to get up.

The floor felt nice and warm, thanks to the under-flooring heating. Feeling much better, she walked over to the window. The sky was still dark; nothing was visible. *Back home, the skies would have lit up by now.* Only a steady whir of rushing automobiles could be heard from a distance. *Today, we must win the cup.* She dialed her mother's mobile and then her grandmother's. As usual, they both answered within two rings. After a brief conversation with both of them, she hung up, feeling more cheerful.

She got ready and woke up Janice, who, for a change, got up immediately. She was also ready within a few minutes, and they both descended the stairs to step into a warm cafeteria humming with the excited buzz of the students. Keith and Abhik were already seated and having their breakfast. Both the professors were also ready. They waved and cheered. Durga felt relaxed and confident.

Breakfast was continental style, and all of them enjoyed drinking glasses of fresh, creamy cold milk, chocolate pudding, deliciously thick muesli, selection of jams, honey in comb with bread (Brot), or bread rolls (Brötchen) with various spreads and toppings.

At precisely 8:30 AM, they were seated in the 'Grand Hall' which was full of several local students. Participants from seven countries – the United States, Germany, India, Australia, Japan, China, and Tunisia – which were shortlisted after an elaborate pre-qualification online test sat as active contestants.

The biggest surprise was the stunningly elegant Quiz Master, Regina Shcaa-Meyer.

"Hi, I am Regina. Welcome to Cologne. I am glad to see you all here. So, shall we begin already? Today, we have seven participating teams from different countries. There will be 50 questions split into five rounds of eight questions. Questions will pertain to Agriculture, Conservation, Environment, Energy & Fuel, Sustainable Transport, and International agreements on Biodiversity. There is no negative marking, so you are free to guess, *Ja?* Let us then go directly to the first round. All the best!" smiled Regina Shcaa-Meyer from the dais.

The Quiz competition began. The first few rounds went super fast. As Durga glanced at the score charts, they were neck-to-neck with the Australian team. Finally, the buzzer round was in, where one had to answer in 10 seconds.

Regina Shcaa-Meyer announced the tie-breaker question...

Durga was delighted. *We have won*, she thought gleefully as she glanced at Abhik, who smiled back and gestured. *May I?* Durga nodded as he pressed the buzzer.

“Correct!! And the Indian team wins this competition. Congratulations!” shouted Regina Shcaa-Meyer as appreciative claps could be heard all around.

Professor Jaywant and Professor Anatanarayan waved a thumbs up, and Durga felt almost weak at the knees as they lifted the cup. Pops of flashbulbs went off, and a ‘selfie’ spree followed. As Janice later put it, they were social media ‘stars’ for one day at least!

It was evening by the time they got back to their rooms. Durga called Bamma and her mother to announce the good news. The following day, the St. George’s School announced a visit to the famed Die Flora, der Botanische Garten Köln, the Botanic Garden of Cologne, followed by a picnic to the Rhine river.

The thin, watery sun was not doing the same job as in India, but the air was bracing and fresh. The mighty Rhine sparkled. Its shores were dotted with German families enjoying a nice, lazy afternoon picnic.

As Professor Jaywant explained, the River Rhine happened to be one of Europe’s major arteries, flowing from the Swiss Alps through diverse and beautiful landscapes in Germany, France, and Holland, where it finally entered the North Sea.

The organizing team from St. George’s was preparing to return to the campus, but goaded by Durga and Abhik, Professor Jaywant and Professor Ananatanarayn yielded and broke away from the group to visit the magnificent Cologne

Cathedral that towered above the roofs and chimneys of the city.

Everyone who visited Cologne felt awe at the tall, majestic Dom cathedral. Legend has it that the great twin spires stood as a highly identifiable navigational landmark for the Allied Forces during World War II, which may be why the cathedral was not destroyed.

After the quick visit to the cathedral, they meandered in the market buying souvenirs and drifted towards Hohenzollern Bridge (Hohenzollernbrücke). They were on the bridge when Janice started snapping pictures. "Hey Diggy, please take a solo of mine with the background of Dom," asked Janice.

Durga nodded and focused her mobile on taking a better picture of Janice and the Dom Cathedral. Suddenly, Durga saw a man talking into his mobile phone, standing to the far left of Janice.

Swiftly, she snapped a picture. *It was Adrian Gerber!*

"Hey, finished? I can't wait to see my picture, Diggy," Janice was still posing.

Durga whirled around. Her professors were busy shopping, while Keith and Abhik were distracted by a skateboarder.

"What's with you?" yelled Janice.

"That man," Durga gasped, "There — look."

“What? Who? Oh, my God.”

“Yes, Jenny, What should we do?”

Janice looked utterly stumped.

“Let’s follow him. Our gang and the professors seem preoccupied. It seems like the perfect time!” Durga said, already picking up pace.

“Heyyy…what the…,” Janice muttered desperately as she cut through the crowd to join Durga.

Durga was racing towards Adrian; she didn’t even stop to apologize as she knocked into a few people in the front. She reached the spot where he stood, buying a ticket. Durga, too, bought two tickets on the same subway train. Janice caught up with Durga, panting.

“Tell me, Diggy, why are we even following Adrian? Isn’t that extremely unsafe?” snapped Janice.

It took thirty seconds for her to realize that Durga was in no mood to answer.

She scrambled frantically along the length of the platform, behind Durga. They both clambered into the train Adrian had boarded, with less than a minute to spare.

Once the train started, Durga heaved a sigh of relief.

“Diggy, you know what we are doing? The professors will be worried about us!”

“Jenny, trust me on this.”

As though on cue, Durga's mobile phone buzzed. It was Professor Jaywant calling.

Durga answered it promptly.

"Hello, Ma'am. We? We just drifted into the next lane, Ma'am, admiring some paintings. Okay, will you wait near the coffee shop? We will come around then. See you in some time."

"Hmm… I hope we can get back soon," muttered Janice.

Adrian settled in a window seat, took out a sheaf of papers, and started reading them.

In a few minutes, he walked towards the exit as Dusseldorf Hauptbahnhof station was coming into view. Everyone stood aside as the doors opened. Adrian got off.

Wrapping their scarves closer to their faces, Durga and Janice followed Adrian, who waved down a taxi. Durga panicked momentarily. An ever-alert Janice, quickly realizing what was happening, hailed the next cab, got in, and requested the kindly looking lady driver to follow the car.

A 10-minute ride later, the taxi arrived at a large suburban house with huge windows and lofts. Durga and Janice got off the cab and stopped at a discreet distance. Adrian alighted from the car and went straight in.

Durga and Janice, thankful that there were no compound walls or dogs, snuck behind some bushes.

“What shall we do?” asked Janice

Durga didn’t say anything.

Just then, Adrian, dressed more informally in jeans teamed with rugged cowboy boots, came out. He stood for some time smoking a cigarette when a small truck came in. Two men got out, handed him a package, and left. After some time, Adrian drove off in a battered car.

“Perfect, Jenny, now that he’s gone, let’s sneak into the house. We may get some clues!”

Durga started moving towards a small side door. Janice followed, marveling at Durga’s newfound courage. Nobody seemed to be about as they pushed the door. It opened into a narrow corridor.

They went down the corridor which led to a flight of steps, and made their way into a well-stocked library. Some books lay on the table. Durga glanced at the covers. Interestingly, most of them were authored by her father! A letter addressed to Adrian Gerber confirmed that it was his house indeed!

Suddenly, the book slipped from Durga’s hands. In the process of grabbing the book, she fell right across the table. Janice almost screamed.

To their amazement, a large section of the floor slid open right before them!

“An underground tunnel! I may have hit a hidden button

when I fell on the table," whispered Durga excitedly. Janice nodded.

Both of them switched on their mobile torches and looked inside. A small stairway of steps was visible.

They went down the steps, shivering as the temperature below became much cooler. Durga also noticed that it was more humid. They walked through another dimly-lit corridor at the end of which was a large wooden door. They pushed, and the door opened. Hearts thumping, Durga and Janice entered and stood transfixed on the spot!

The hall was well-lit and large, filled with many terrariums of all sizes, shapes, and compositions! Many organically shaped vessels of different types of glass or acrylic filled with a wide variety of plant life were mounted on the walls, or stood alongside their microscopic habitats. Durga and Janice started taking pictures of each. Finally, Durga came to stand near a large, free-standing, egg-shaped, floor-to-ceiling structure containing the 'Nymphaea thermarum,' the smallest water lily in the world.

"My God, this is a kind of museum, Jenny! Here's where he is hiding all the stolen germplasm! Adrian has created different atmospheric conditions in each terrarium to match the species' requirements."

"Don't touch anything," warned Durga.

Suddenly, they heard some noise outside and froze.

"Let's get out of here," whispered Durga, and Janice

nodded. They managed to get out of the tunnel, into the library, and towards the road. Janice had resourcefully requested the taxi driver to wait by paying her extra. The taxi was still there. The girls heaved a sigh of relief. Within a few minutes, they were back at the Düsseldorf Hauptbahnhof.

Luckily for them, there was a train to Cologne in the next three minutes. At 6:45 PM, they got off at Cologne Hauptbahnhof and ran towards the café near the Hollenzoren bridge to meet their professors and friends as promised. The entire expedition had taken less than 30 minutes! *Only in Germany can this happen. The efficiency of the systems was too impressive,* thought Durga.

Professor Jaywant and Professor Anantanarayan looked in their direction and nodded. They were too engrossed in looking at some travel brochures.

"Ah, there you are. We ordered for you both as well," exclaimed Keith and Abhik. Their eyes were full of questions.

"Guys, we went to Adrian Gerber's house..."

"What???"

Durga and Janice recounted their adventure elaborately, describing the terrariums as Abhik and Keith listened in rapt attention.

"Well, the real stuff begins now," finished Durga.

All of them fist-bumped a *Yes*.

There was just one more day of sightseeing left to do in Cologne. They visited the famous Imhoff-Schokoladenmuseum, the Waterside museum devoted to chocolate. It housed exhibits tracing the 3,000-year history of chocolate, from the time of the Aztecs to today. Despite their schedule, they were so enamored by the views of chocolate that they stepped into the Chocolat Grand Café inside the museum. It had a great view of the Rhine with a 30-meter-long panorama window that gave the viewer the feeling of sitting directly above the water. Hot drinking chocolate, chocolate tarts, chocolate fondants, crêpes, fresh waffles, tarte flambé, salads...the array was endless.

"Let's order like there's no tomorrow," Janice declared with an air of pomp, and for once, everyone agreed wholeheartedly.

As their plane touched down in Hyderabad, they all cheered loudly. A large group of friends and school staff stood outside with flowers and placards proclaiming a hearty welcome.

Principal Roy personally congratulated them. "This is an unforgettable moment for Magnolia. In light of this glorious achievement, I award the APJ group 100 house points!"

The day seemed perfect. The best part was that their House Points were restored. Even though they still trailed 50 points behind the CV Raman team, they felt much better.

Chapter Sixteen

A Time of Trial

"Wow, one full weekend of a proper holiday! I couldn't have asked for more!!" exclaimed Janice dramatically as they stretched out on the grass, soaking in the sunshine.

Durga, Janice, Keith, and Abhik had elected to stay back at school while many students packed and went on short trips. They still had their herbariums to complete, as Professor Anantanarayan had reminded them gravely. However, nobody was in the mood to listen to her this time.

"Guys, we need to go to Araku now. How do we do it?" asked Durga.

"I have an idea. We could ask to go to Araku to complete the herbarium," said Keith.

"Great idea!"

"I am sure they will send somebody with us," said Janice glumly.

"Of course. But we can easily give this person the slip and go up the mountain," suggested Abhik.

"Now, that sounds like a plan," said Janice.

They collectively sent the email request to Principal Roy.

"Hey guys, we got the permission to go to Araku. Pack sensibly," Durga announced ecstatically, the next day.

Maybe it was because of the recent wins, but the Principal's permission had come through very quickly. They managed to get the required two days' permission to visit Araku Valley. The only downside was that Professor Jaywant was accompanying them.

However, Janice was confident of finding a way to give her the slip.

"Adrian, KM switched on the device, and we received the image. It looks like an ancient parchment," said Bosch showing Adrian the image.

Adrian's heartbeat quickened. *Could this be Dr. Harish's secret quest? The weapon?*

"By the way, I have traced the recent security breach. It came from a laptop belonging to Abhik, a close friend of Durga's," Bosch was still speaking.

Adrian's eyes twitched.

"Where were they in the last few days?"

Bosch checked his iPad.

"They were here in Cologne! For some school quiz!" said Bosch disbelievingly. Adrian merely sighed.

"Check the security camera feed for the last two weeks right now!"

Bosch did as told, and reported, "Two boys entered this facility and the terrarium four days ago. We didn't get a report because nothing was touched, so it was assumed to be kids fooling around. This is the first time it ever happened!" muttered Bosch nervously.

"It only takes once…we are becoming complacent. Check the feed closely. Track that boy Abhik's laptop and tell me what they are up to?"

Bosch grabbed his mobile, giving terse instructions to his IT team. A few moments later…

"Adrian, you are right! They seem to be girls. Same height as Durga and Janice. We tracked that boy's laptop, and they are researching A-raku or Araku Valley near Vizag city, in South India."

Adrian was thinking fast. *Durga might have unraveled the parchment clue. That means she probably knows about the final secret.*

"Let's go there asap. Meanwhile, follow their every move."

Durga was reading her favorite book. Janice was

watching a video on Araku Valley.

Durga's mobile trilled, and she picked it up. It was her grandmother.

"Amma, I have to give you some harsh news! You have to be prepared for it mentally."

Durga's heart raced. *Is it Nanna? Please, God, let it not be about his health.* She prayed in that instant.

"What is it, Bamma?" asked Durga, hoping she sounded calm. Her knees were shaking already. Janice looked up from her video, sensing the tension in Durga's voice.

What? asked Janice, gesturing. Durga put her mobile on the loudspeaker.

"I am heartbroken to tell you..that-that we have lost…."

There was silence on the line. Durga waited, her heart pounding in her ears.

"Lost the case, Amma. Your father is no longer the King. Dhyaneshwara Raju will be the Legal Heir to the throne," declared her grandmother in a resolute voice.

Durga's first reaction was one of relief. That her dad was okay. But immediately after, she felt the blow. *My God!*

"B-but Bamma, this is brutal! How did this happen?"

"Dhyana came up with some lies, that Rajasaheb, your grandfather, was not mentally unstable when he anointed your father, Hari, as the King. Now that your father has lost his memory and you are a girl, and under age, he argued that the inheritance has to pass to the next in the line. And he is next in the line."

"What will be the consequence of this, Bamma?" asked Durga.

"Well, we have to give away everything, including our Devdi. Return the crown and the sword since you will cease to be the Princess. We have to leave everything here. Tomorrow is his coronation. We are not even invited."

"My God! Give away our home? But…but..."

"Don't worry. Your Chinnanna has invited us to stay at the Errada Beach House at Vizag. I am taking your father there. Your mother will join us too. She thinks if there was some way to prove that Rajasaheb intended your father to be King in the letter or a will, we could contest the whole thing. Also, your father will have to heal fully. Only then can he be considered for the title. Anyway, right now, it seems we cannot do much. Try not to worry too much. Just be calm. This, too, shall pass. In the meantime, we are thinking of ways to counter this. We will not go quietly into the night. We will most certainly fight. By the way, there will be a media splash. Don't pay too much attention to it,"

For the first time, Durga heard a sound of despair in her grandmother's voice.

"Take care," her grandmother rang off with a sound that was like a sob.

Durga collapsed on the chair, feeling absolutely despondent. Janice sat next to her, holding her hand. They stayed that way for a long time.

"So, here's the Princess Nobody. You know that Durga has been stripped of her title. Ha ha. My father is the King, and I am the Princess!" Akanksha's mocking voice rang out in the classroom.

Everyone was looking curiously at Durga. It was clear that the news was all out on social media platforms. Abhik and Keith were constantly tracking this.

The week was getting worse, with people openly staring at Durga and whispering. She was stricken. In the midst of all this, the election for Cultural Secretary was on. As much as Janice, Keith, and Abhik tried to cheer Durga up and hounded her to participate in the campaigning, she was too far gone this time. As a result, Akanksha won without practically any competition!

Nobody dared to say anything to Durga as they sat in the library quietly. Durga's mobile vibrated. *You don't need to be a Princess to act like one. You ARE one. Don't forget your quest. Don't get distracted. There are too many things at stake.*

The message was from a number that was not from her contact list. Durga looked up, confused.

"Abhi, can you track this number?"

"Let me try."

"No use, D. It was probably sent by a simple device with a rechargeable SIM. That's why I am not able to track it."

Durga sighed. Nothing seemed to be going right anymore.

"Why should I bother? It's not my concern anymore. I am NOT the Princess anymore. It doesn't matter now," replied Durga sadly.

"Don't talk like that, D. I am quite fed up of you, poor-mouthing yourself all the time," glowered Janice.

"And what do you know? Passing judgments? Put yourself in my shoes. Then you will know!" glared Durga.

"Will you two stop it? D, take it easy. You are going through a lot right now. Jen, please be gentle. Whatever you are doing will not work," beseeched Keith.

Janice and Durga continued to sulk. Abhik sat silently. Even Nibbles was quiet, sensing the tension.

Just then, they spotted Professor Jaywant approaching them with some papers in her hand.

"Hello, why are we all sulking?" she enquired.

Durga, Janice, Keith, and Abhi greeted her perfunctorily.

"Nothing is going right, Professor," the sob in Durga's voice was apparent.

Professor Jaywant nodded with understanding.

"I heard the news. It is difficult to understand this at your age, but life is like this. It's full of ups and downs, and sometimes things don't go as planned. It's easy to feel discouraged and down when faced with setbacks, but remember that every setback is an opportunity to bounce back stronger than before. You are all strong and capable, and you have the power within you to overcome any obstacle. When things don't go as planned, take a deep breath and consider what you can learn from the experience. Every successful person has faced failures along the way, but what sets him or her apart is the ability to bounce back and keep going. So, don't give up, keep trying, and never lose hope. You are all amazing young people with incredible potential. What you have done with your detention is simply awe-inspiring! Believe in yourself, stay positive, and keep moving forward. The future is bright, and you can achieve anything you set your mind to. So, bounce back stronger and brighter than before, and show the world what you are capable of!" Professor Jaywant spoke passionately. Her eyes glistened with tears.

There was a profound silence.

Each of them knew that Professor Jaywant had refused to go to Cambridge even though she had won a full scholarship and had instead, decided to stay back to take care of her aged parents. She didn't marry for the same reason. Her life was inspirational enough!

"Thank you, Professor," they all said in unison.

"Cheer up," she gave them all a high-five and proceeded to her classroom.

By mutual agreement, they went their own ways. Janice went to her dance class. Keith and Abhik went back to their rooms. Durga decided to take a walk.

"Amma, Durgamma, I have a stomachache. Can you give me some medicine? I am Swaroopa, from the cleaning department, Amma."

Durga looked around to see a woman standing with a pitiful expression. She was in pain.

Durga rummaged through her bag, brought out the herbal powder, mixed it with water from her bottle, and gave it to her. Durga made her sit and rest there for a few minutes.

"Thank you, Durgamma. Ah, the pain is gone! May God bless you. You have a healing touch in your hands. Don't worry about what people say. You are a born princess, and you will always be one."

Durga smiled and helped the lady get up, who seemed to have recovered considerably. She slowly went on her way.

Returning to her room, Durga flung her bag on the bed. Her head was buzzing with thoughts. It was as though she couldn't control them. She tried her mom's number, which seemed busy.

Restlessly, she started pacing up and down. *What if those*

poisonous plants get into Adrian's hands? Clearly, Akanksha wasn't so talented at figuring out the clues. The parchment had already reached Adrian and his gang. It was only a matter of time.

Her mobile trilled, and she looked at it to see her friends calling her for dinner.

Though she was in no mood for it, she got up and reached the dining hall. Janice, Keith, and Abhik greeted her enthusiastically. They were trying their best to lift her spirits.

"Okay, we are starting tomorrow for Araku. Everything is set," Janice was hollering away in her usual loud fashion.

"I have the hiking boots ready, Jen."

"My chair has got extra wheels," boasted Abhik.

Go where you're lookin', and look where you're goin' squealed Nibbles.

"How can she figure out what line to say, Abhi?" asked Keith, marveling.

Durga smiled.

Did it matter that she was no longer the Princess to her friends? Did it matter to that woman who had asked her help?

The answer was as clear as day to her.

Chapter Seventeen

The Forbidden Trail

Durga stopped abruptly in her tracks. Her heart pounded loudly in her ears as she willed herself to turn around. *Was someone following her?* There was no one. *Perhaps, it's all my imagination.* The timing seemed perfect since Professor Jaywant had suddenly felt sick, and their day's expedition was put off to the next day. Janice was sleeping soundly, with Abhik and Keith in the next room. Durga had slipped out. She just wanted to do this alone.

The location was indeed a trekker's paradise. All along the path were stout, thick brown, overgrown trees of Regi berries, the Naramamidi variety of wild mango that grew in these parts, and sweet lime trees laden with fruit. There were many thick shrubs with tiny bunches of delicious-looking purple berries all around. Ripe Jackfruit hanging heavy from tubby trunks that resembled large eastern oaks let off a rich, sweetish scent that hung in the air. Every inch of the ground was covered with thick, mossy green vegetation, leading to an occasional crop of creamy-white mushrooms. A swarm of tiny flies buzzed incessantly around her face. Bushy-tailed squirrels darted across her path, playfully chasing one another, unmindful of her presence.

All she needed was two more hours. Her intention was clear. She needed to retrace the path to find the temple. Then she could come back with her friends.

The green of the valley distracted her for a moment. It was a nice vantage point. From atop Gali Konda, she could see the magnificent sweep of the surging and dipping hillocks of the Araku Valley. Due to the high elevation of Gali Konda, rainfall was copious, and therefore, the valley consisted of mixed deciduous forests with a luxuriant growth of orchids, ferns, and epiphytes that blossomed into myriad colored flowers that hung gracefully from large trees, sometimes covered with thick, velvety moss.

Suddenly, Durga spotted the plant with light violet plum-colored flowers - Emilia reddyi!

Ah, the twig! So, I am on the right track.

The wind howled around her eerily. *Everything here seemed undisturbed. Why is the fruit on the trees unpicked?* she wondered. This was highly unusual considering the tribal settlement that was somewhere in the area. And yet, the trail seemed functional enough.

Suddenly, Durga caught a movement. She cautiously moved behind a big mango tree. From the corner of her eye, she could see a thick Vakkai berry bush move ever so slightly. The silence was deafening.

Something fell with a soft thud next to Durga; she screamed and raced wildly, and Janice, incredibly clad in a

A path less traveled awaits...

designer camouflage outfit, sprang up from behind the 'shivering' berry bush.

"J-J-Jenny!" gasped Durga.

For a moment, it looked as though Janice might faint. She clutched her throat and made a choking noise.

"Diggy! Oh, thank goodness – Diggy!" Janice slid to the ground. "You almost killed me. I need some water. I hope I am not dead," she whispered hoarsely as she drew a sipper from her backpack and took a deep swig.

"FAR FROM IT! WHAT ARE YOU DOING HERE?"

"Well, I know you. You, being you – would most certainly try and do this exciting thing all by yourself and very selfishly too and then later give me some sentimental-boo-hoo stuff like..."

Durga tried to punch her, but as usual, Janice was too fast for her.

"...And I, being I – decided to keep an eye on you. After much thought, I decided to wear these camos so that I could 'blend' into the scenario, for I dare not draw your attention," Janice concluded solemnly.

"Diggy, I have some more news," Janice uttered the words cautiously.

"What is that?" grunted Durga.

"Keith."

"Yes…what about him?" glared Durga.

"He-He's here as well."

"Sorry, D, I am right here," Keith came out of hiding, looking embarrassed.

I am also here. I am also here, squealed Nibbles in a Clint Eastwood accent.

Janice giggled. Durga sighed.

"What about Abhik?"

"I am here too," said a voice as Durga turned to see a small camera pinned on Keith's shirt.

"Really? Any more to come? No? Good. I am actually very relieved that you are all with me. Let's go," declared Durga.

"Okay. How do we hunt for the temple? Which direction to go?" wondered Janice.

"We have Google for that. Not to worry, go straight and turn left" Abhik started giving directions, and they set off along the woody landscape.

They neared the precincts of an abandoned temple.

The place seemed deserted.

Slowly, they entered the sculptured threshold filled with tufts of swollen, green moss dotted with occasional flowers. Large ferns and bunches of fragrant wild purple orchids hung over the archway.

"Where is the entrance?" wondered Janice trying to peek through the trees and the rocks.

A column of rough-hewn rocks fallen in certain places, still holding up a pair of decaying doors ornamented with darkened metal knobs, came into view.

They soon pried the door with knives and cutters and stepped inside.

A stone-cut courtyard supported by several sculpted pillars enclosed the temple on four sides.

The courtyard itself was surprisingly neat.

A large black stone carving of Nandi at the far end of the courtyard sat on a sculpted base with four carved pillars.

In the middle was the Garbhagriha, *the sanctum sanctorum*. Sunlight streamed through steadily. The air was fresh, and the weather cool.

They fanned out taking pictures.

"I have a feeling that we are being watched," murmured Keith uncomfortably.

Durga and Janice nodded.

"Let's go inside the garbhagriha," suggested Durga.

As they entered, they wrinkled their noses as a wave of the nauseating smell of bat droppings hit them.

The garbhagriha was, as per the Hindu tradition, a windowless and sparsely lit chamber.

In the center was an elliptical linga.

A steady plop plop of water falling cut through the stillness.

"Is there water somewhere?" asked Janice checking the ground with her torch.

But the floor was quite dry.

"Guys look," said Keith ever so quietly, pointing his torch to the ceiling.

From the ceiling of the garbhagriha, a carved stone lotus hung down, and from its middle, a crystal stream of water was falling over the linga in a gentle, steady stream.

"Where is the water coming from," exclaimed Janice trying to peer at the ceiling.

"Maybe a freshwater spring that emerges from under the temple has been channeled to flow out through the lotus?

Seems like a perfect example of ancient hydraulic engineering," said Keith, spellbound.

Durga examined the sculpted walls flashing her torch. *There could be a clue here.* She decided to take a closer look.

"Guys, come here."

Janice and Keith rushed to Durga's side.

"Guys, I need to climb a bit. Can you help me?" Janice and Keith groaned as they lifted her up.

There was a figure of a young priest holding a staff and bowing to a lady, who held a small floral twig in her hands. A single palasa flower. Turned to the other side.

Palasa - the auspicious flower! Instinctively, Durga felt the outline of the flower. In the center was a small knot.

She pressed it.

All of a sudden, one section of the wall right in front of them slid aside noiselessly.

Durga jumped down excitedly.

'Wow!' they all exclaimed.

Peering in, they could see a pitch-black passage, barely wide enough for an adult to get through, leading to a curved staircase.

Nibbles started whistling the *For a few dollars more*, movie track.

"Hahaha, Nibbles! Okay. A cowboy tune, How appropriate! Let's do it," said Janice taking a deep breath dramatically as she placed a foot in the passage.

Suddenly, with a whir, something landed at their feet.

Terror-stricken, Janice shrieked.

Keith stood petrified.

Durga fought back the bile that was rising in her throat to look at the object.

It was an arrow!

She whirled around. And screamed in horror.

Twenty men, bodies smeared with charcoal black, in tribal attires, and crowns made of colorful plumes, stood with their bows aloft!

She noticed that one man was kneeling in front of her.

"Durgavathi Rani Sahiba. Vijayaosthu."

At this, the entire band of tribals bowed low.

He was addressing her, greeting her.

"My name is Eraka Raju. I am the head of Akku. We are a tribal clan of warriors living in this valley, who have sworn to protect this temple as per the command of our King of Vijayanagaram. Now you are our queen," he said in heavily accented Telugu.

Durga was still tongue-tied.

"How come we never heard you coming in?" asked a perplexed Janice.

Eraka Raju smiled gently.

"You will never hear us. We are like the wind and the shadow. We are the invisible men of war," he said.

"Did you know my father?" asked Durga, finally mustering up her courage.

"Yes, Rani Saheba. We did. And I am ashamed that I am alive today when my master is hurt," Erika Raju's eyes glistened.

Durga was thinking quickly. *These guys could come in handy. And they can keep watch.*

"Will you help us then?"

"Your word is our command!"

"Then go. Keep watch." said Durga in a commanding voice.

In the blink of an eye, they were gone!

"Wow, Diggy, that was pretty impressive," approved Janice.

Durga nodded, wondering from where she had found her commanding demeanor all of a sudden!

"Okay, let's get on with it."

Keith and Janice nodded, and carefully climbed inside the passage.

The minute they entered. The panel shut! They switched on their torches.

"Don't worry. I can still see you," Abhik's voice gave them courage.

"Did they have sensors even in those times?" wondered Keith.

"More likely that our weight would have triggered it to shut," said Durga.

The steps seemed to wind into sharp inversions and they felt like they were in a 360-degrees VR roller coaster.

"You know it feels right out of some Pirates of the Caribbean movie," said Keith animatedly.

Nibbles broke into the *Pirates of the Caribbean* movie tune.

Janice giggled. Durga laughed.

Finally, the flight of steps descended to a small room with a very low ceiling.

"Now what?" wondered Keith.

Durga, after careful examination, realized that the floor had two perfectly fitted rectangular stone slabs.

She looked up. The ceiling had elaborate carvings of trees, flowers, and shrubs.

Durga felt excitement tingling in her every nerve.

She stared at the carvings for a few minutes in the torch's light.

There it was. The faint outline of Thespesia populnea.

"Ah-ha, the Umbrella Tree…" whispered Abhik.

"Yes. Thespesios means divine in Greek. It's an old plant from ancient times," Durga murmured as she found its flower, which resembled a tulip.

She felt around the flower. Swiftly, the flower slid inside, revealing a small box-like space.

Inside was a small, circular wheel-like brass lever. She started to turn it.

The stone slabs swung open.

Chapter Eighteen

The World Within

"Diggy, you are marvelous!" exclaimed Janice and Keith.

Durga smiled. The exhilaration was pumping through her. After another flight of steps, they came to a small landing. Once again, they wondered how the air inside was still fresh! Towering before them was a pair of massive doors closed tight shut. Two giant serpents were sculpted on either side of the doors. On the top was a royal coat of arms belonging to the regent of the Kingdom of Vijayanagaram.

"Oh sweet lord, what next?" fidgeted Janice.

"They are made of solid gold! Look," pointed Keith from behind.

They scrutinized the door closely. It had intricate sculptures with inlay work of semi-precious stones and gold.

"How do we open it?" asked Janice.

"Hmmm...give me a few minutes," murmured Durga.

As she examined the carvings, she found the sloka!

Yattadagre vishameva parinaamemritopapam

tatsukham saattvikam proktamaatmabuddhiprasaadajam

"Guys, it's the same sloka. From the parchment." said Durga and read it aloud.

"My God!" they chorused, jumping back as the doors rumbled open.

A single squawk of a bird shattered the stillness.

Adrian stood still for a while and motioned his team to stop.

The mid-noon sun had come on. The heat was climbing once again.

Bosch looked uneasily at the thriving landscape. From a botanical point of view, it was intriguing. A part of him longed to explore. He fought down the feeling reluctantly.

What was Adrian waiting for? He thought impatiently, as he hoisted his gun on his shoulder, expecting the worst.

Just as he turned around, arrows whizzed past him, missing him by inches.

Petrified, he swung low on his knees.

Adrian had done the same.

And maybe that's what saved them.

All three of their men lay sprawled on the ground. *Dead.*

Tribals! Well, I have some tricks of my own, Adrian thought grimly, as he uncorked a tear gas cylinder and hurled it in the direction of the tribals.

Taking cover behind the blanket of smoke released by the cylinder, Adrian and Bosch ran to the temple and hid in the courtyard.

Eraka Raju smiled. *Come. Come. We are waiting!*

"Do you think the sound waves triggered some mechanism? I heard that it was in-built in some of our ancient temples. Wow!" Abhik was marveling at the sight, watching from his laptop.

"Yes. That must be it," said Keith, smiling.

Durga, Janice, and Keith entered, slowly climbing down a few steps.

"Do you think we can get back in time, Diggy?" asked Janice worriedly.

"I don't know," said Durga slowly. Janice gulped.

Only Keith seemed happy and unaffected.

The golden sculpted pillars studded with diamonds and gems glittered in the light, creating a gentle radiance in the grand hall. They saw another garbhagriha in the center.

Nibbles started singing a traditional Telugu song.

Janice at once started striking Bharatanatyam poses imitating those on the pillars. Keith snapped some pictures.

Light and fresh air came from spaces between the intricate stone sculptures in the high walls.

"It's so fresh!" exclaimed Keith.

"This temple is on a mountain, right? They may have constructed it such that a part of it would be open from the side to let in fresh air and light," suggested Janice.

"Very nice deduction, Jenny," approved Durga.

The entire area was a square with four entrances protruding in four directions. However, the doors were sealed shut.

In front of the garbhagriha, on the sculpted ceiling, was another elaborate carving of a lotus from which a steady stream of water was disappearing into a small tank shaped like a triangle with radiating smaller triangles. Encircling it was a sculpture of circles with lotus petals. "Guys, this is the Sri Chakra," whispered Abhik. "What does that mean?" asked Keith as Janice and Durga circled in wonder.

"It's a powerful symbol of the Goddess," replied Abhik

"Okay. And the water?"

"Keith, it is probably the same stream of water…that means we are now right below the Shiva temple, several feet deep inside the mountain. See how clear the water is... and there are tortoises and fish too," exclaimed Durga.

"Amazing, they did this stuff without computers?" exclaimed a dazed Abhik, who video-recorded everything.

The most magnificent of all was the garbhagriha. Inside was the statue of Narasimha, the fiery-eyed, fourth incarnation of Vishnu. In his upper left hand, he held a conch, his upper right hand held a chakra or a disk, while his major left hand and right hand were killing the demon king Hiranyakashipu. The friends gazed admiringly at the sculpture, which was so defined and awe-inspiring.

So far, the clues add up. Nanna's letter too mentioned Nrusimha. Durga checked the statue for clues but found none.

"There are no bells. All temples usually have, na?" observed Keith.

"Yes. But this does not seem like a usual temple where devotees were admitted," offered Janice.

Durga grinned discreetly. Both of them were getting along famously with their own 'discoveries.'

"But what is the next step?" probed Janice.

"I need some time, guys," said Durga.

Keith and Janice nodded and went off on their own to look at things.

Durga studied the walls on all sides. As she was looking, her foot hit a sharp edge. Groaning, she reached down to rub her foot. That's when she saw it. The floor was elaborately carved with various motifs into a veritable carpet.

Her eyes settled on the motif of a flower she most definitely knew.

"Ashoka," she cried. Keith and Janice came running.

Keith looked at it for a few moments and shook his head.

"Sorry, D. Thanks to your training for the past few months, I can tell that this is NOT an Ashoka flower."

"Okay, guys. Polyalthia longifolia is the False Ashoka tree."

"Ohhh...aww..."

"Yes. The real one is very ancient and well-documented in our scriptures in a very auspicious way. Here is the perfect example."

Keith, Abhik, and Janice started listening with rapt attention.

Durga proceeded to explain a bit.

"Its scientific name is Saraca asoca or sometimes referred to as Saraca indica, and belongs to the Caesalpinioideae subfamily of the legume family. It has elegant foliage and fragrant bright orange-yellow flowers that present themselves in heavy, lush bunches. You know, there is a charming Indian belief that trees will flower only in places where a woman's foot has trod and another, which asserts that a tree will bloom more vigorously if kicked by a young lady! And I did just that," said Durga examining the carving.

It was the figure of a lady standing under the tree in full blossom. She was holding a branch in her right hand. Durga traced her fingers over the spot where the drawing ended.

The tree seemed to emerge into a small carving near the water tank. Once again, Durga looked inside the tank. The surface water seemed clear, revealing the fish and the tortoises but the bottom was muddy and dark. Nothing was visible.

She started checking the radiating points of the triangles. Unexpectedly, her hand struck a small knob-like thing. She pressed it, and lo!

The water tank had disappeared, and in its place was a gaping black hole leading further down.

"Geez, see this…" shouted Durga. *Is it a way to get out?* She wondered.

By the time Janice and Keith turned, there was a loud noise….

Adrian and Bosch, rushed in holding small, compact pistols.

"Don't move and put your hands where I can see them,"

growled Bosch menacingly.

Durga, Keith, and Janice put up their hands.

Durga had already moved her foot ever so slowly to hit the knob near the water tank again. She saw from the corner of her eyes that the gaping hole was gone, and the water tank had come back on.

Adrian noticed Durga's slight movement and rushed towards her. However, he couldn't figure out if anything was amiss.

For a moment, he looked at her. Durga stared back steadily.

"We need to hurry, Adrian. *Klappe zu, Affe tot* (End of story). There is plenty to do," said Bosch coming towards them.

"Okay, Durga, if you tell us where the poison garden is, we will let your friends go. By the way, we found your friend Abhik, who hacked into our systems. Now we have complete control of his laptop. Look, you can see for yourself," said Bosch in an utterly menacing soft voice and showed his mobile where Durga could see Abhik tied up in his chair, looking dejected.

Durga screamed. "You are an animal!"

"Don't worry about calling us names. It is you who led us here. Breaking into our facility, snooping on us in Cologne," said Bosch.

"Okay. So, where is the poison garden? The faster you tell, the better it will be for all of us here," threatened Adrian.

"I don't know. I haven't cracked it yet," said Durga.

Adrian came over and stood near Durga menacingly.

"Well, do it now, or your friend here gets it," said Bosch aiming the revolver at Janice's head.

"WHAT...!"

Just then, a loud bang startled them all. It was followed by clouds of smoke that stung their eyes. Out of it emerged Eraka Raju and the Akku warriors.

A single shot burst out.

Durga, horrified, screamed. Janice and Keith collapsed to the floor.

A pool of blood was quickly gathering around Janice. Her eyes were shut.

Keith lay injured on the ground.

Durga was screaming, tears running down her cheeks.

"JANICE, JANICE, KEITH, NO..."

In a series of fast movements, Bosch overpowered Eraka Raju and pinned him to the ground. It was just a matter of seconds before Eraka Raju overpowered Bosch. Unperturbed by it all, Adrian started shooting at will.

Many Akku warriors fell down injured. Some shots hit

the gem-studded pillars, making them shower out on the floor.

Adrian and Bosch rushed forward to pick up some of the precious diamonds and gems.

I need to safeguard the secret of the poison garden. Need to escape from here. Need to save Jenny and Keith.

Durga felt the moment.

Eraka Raju was already getting up and looking in her direction. She gestured to him to take care of her friends.

He nodded.

Durga pressed the knob with her foot. The water tank disappeared, and a large hole appeared in its place.

Without thinking, she jumped.

The ceiling closed over her!

Falling. Falling.

It seemed like a long time before Durga fell with a thud.

The bottom of the tunnel was filled with some kind of soft moss. Durga brushed off her tears and switched on the torch. She started walking. After several twists and turns, the tunnel opened into a vast, open space.

Durga clambered out. However, it was not exactly an open space. It was another cavern formed by the crumbling of its roof.

She looked around in complete wonderment. All around her was an abundance of flowering plants, creepers of various types, and trees laden with fruit. Birds sang sonorously, afternoon sunrays cast gentle shadows on the ground. Throughout this scenic landscape, meandered a crystal clear stream that ran the length of the cavern and disappeared into other caves that branched off from the main one.

From the location, she guessed she might now be on the other side of the mountain.

The wide-open space sprung sidewards from inside the mountain. She had read about locations like these, like the recently discovered Son Doong Cave in Vietnam, a remarkable natural wonder, home to a river, jungles, and entire cave ecosystems.

A world within a world.

Chapter Nineteen

Much More Than Meets the Eye!

Her father had mentioned several times that cave formations were not unusual in this geography, but somehow, this one didn't feel like an ordinary cave. It was like someone or somebody had created this place over many decades.

The breathtaking scenery was almost like one of those picturesque screensavers. At the center stood a moon bridge!

The moon bridge cut out of rough-hewn rock lay over a small canal of still, gleaming water. The high arch and its reflection below formed a perfect circle.

From the bridge hung luxuriant green fronds and orchids in varied hues, all forming a profusion of colors in the waters below.

Durga ran to the bridge and gingerly stepped on it, wondering if the ancient structure would collapse under her weight. But it turned out to be quite sturdy.

The path snaked out in one direction just beyond where the bridge ended.

Durga came off the bridge and checked her compass.

It was pointing South.

Determined, she set off.

One thing that struck her was the absolute stillness. The air was damp. There was not even a single bird chirping.

Durga shivered involuntarily.

The lone, winding path was curving softly into turns amidst dense vegetation.

Finally, at a distance, she could see a sizeable dark mound.

Coming closer, she saw the mound was not one unit but a series of pointy knolls filled with plants.

She first noticed Cerbera odollam, popularly called the 'suicide tree.'

There was the bushy green Ruta graveolens, commonly called Rue and Euphorbia. She knew brushing against them or touching the sap could give the person a nasty rash.

She recognized May Apple (Podophyllum spp.) and Amanita phalloides or the 'Death cap mushroom.'

The mounds culminated into a large pentacle formation filled with plants with beautiful rosy flowers and red berries.

In the center was Rafflesia arnoldii, considered the biggest individual flower in the world. It was letting off an unpleasant, irritating odor.

Going further, she found the crab's eye, 'the deadly love bean,' known scientifically as Abrus precatorius. Its seeds contained abrin, an extremely poisonous chemical.

There was the Upas tree, Antiaris toxicaria, also known as the Poison Arrow Tree. This tree was notorious for its poisonous sap, which was used by ancient tribes to coat the tips of their arrows for hunting and warfare.

In another array, she identified the Strychnine tree, Strychnos nux-vomica, another poisonous tree native to India. Its seeds contained strychnine, a potent neurotoxin that caused convulsions and death in high doses. This was primarily used for poisoning and assassination.

She realized this was a group of the deadliest plants in the world.

Using these, one could wipe out a sizeable human population without leaving a trace! The perfect killing machines! Why did her ancestors breed this place?

Durga remembered her father telling her about how ancient Indian kings used poisons as a part of warfare. Indian herbal medicine also requires poisonous plants. The Sushruta Samhita, India's ancient medical treatise, was supposed to have an entire chapter on poisonous plants.

She looked at the path freshly, wondering if it was a good

idea to continue. But something inside her pushed her, and she decided to carry on. The pathway seemed to circle until it stopped. Right there was a small pond with dark, stagnant water. Durga circumnavigated the pond. At the pond's edge was a single stone sculpture of a lotus. It was very intricate.

Durga marveled at the sculpture. Idly, she passed her hands around the lotus petals. Suddenly, there was a loud snap followed by a loud rumble.

She screamed, taken aback by the loud sound. Slowly, she opened her eyes and willed herself to look at it again; there was no pond! In its place was a curved sliding tunnel.

I don't like sliding tunnels even in the water parks. She gulped and jumped. She slid down, screaming as the tunnel took several turns before dropping her on to hard ground.

Groaning, she looked around. She was in front of a large rectangular cave-like structure with sealed rock doors emblazoned with her regency's royal coat of arms. *What would be behind those?* she wondered nervously.

The first task was to open the doors. She got up, dusting off the gravel from her dress.

One lone sculpture of a Baobab tree spread across the doors.

Adansonia suarezensis.

The outstanding feature was that its leaves were large and smooth and described as digitate — five leaflets radiating from a central point.

She looked for the central point and pressed it. The doors swung open.

She stepped inside. The roomy space was dark, the floor covered with downy, soft moss. She switched on her pocket torch, and in the light, saw giant copper vessels, their mouths closed with leather-bound strings that seemed intact and placed randomly.

She tried to lift one of the covers; fine dust rose, and she sneezed.

Covering her mouth and nose with a small tissue, she looked inside.

Inside the pots were little carved boxes filled with seeds of various kinds.

Ancient seeds! Were they also poisonous?

Her gut instinct was telling her otherwise. Nothing here seemed poisonous.

She had read that seeds have long-duration viability. There were already many examples. Judean date palm seed about 2,000 years old, recovered from excavations in Israel, had germinated. Similarly, a 1,300-year-old sacred lotus retrieved from a dry lake bed in China had been restored.

All of a sudden, she saw a faint glow beyond the walls. Curious, she looked to see if there was some way down. Stairs cut of rock curved around the walls of the cave room leading below. Durga climbed down. Slowly, the steps became narrower and narrower, leading her into another cavern that was glowing. Even the floor was aglow with a greenish hue. It was breathtaking.

Bioluminescent fungus.

This is all very nice, but is there a way out? Durga wondered as she started checking the walls frantically.

Tucked away in the far corner of the cave, she found what she was looking for — the carving of a door on the wall. Looking closer, she realized that it wasn't rock but metal. It reminded her of the copper plates. She squatted on the floor and examined the carving. It was tightly shut.

How to open this? Ahh..the Melakartas! They might do the trick.

She sang a few ragas. But nothing worked. A wave of utter desperation rolled over her. The memory of Janice and Keith lying in a pool of blood flashed before her, and she cried out, huge sobs welling out of her. She lay there utterly despondent until she gathered herself again. With renewed vigour, she jumped up and took a look at the door again. Then... she saw the Sunflower.

Ah, Suryakantham raga melakarta!

Even as she started to sing, there was a loud metallic clanking of something moving!

A small space had popped open in the wall! Large

enough for an adult to crawl through it. She could see the sunlight outside.

A wave of relief flowed through her as she gathered her things and crawled on her stomach. She tumbled out into the open space, panting.

Her eyes took some time to adjust to the bright light outside. She was standing on some sort of a starry pyramid. Though there were no steps, the diagonally protruding sculpted triangle-like structures would make the climb easy. She was already halfway up.

Durga climbed on. The peak was flat and round, covered with a sculptured manhole like the ones she had seen in Japan; only this was much bigger, with many circular holes. She looked down through the holes, which were quite large and offered a perfect view of the inside. A vast landscape lay below her, filled with various flowering plants in myriad colors. Durga wrenched the manhole open in one single movement.

Looking down, she felt faint. It was fairly deep. *I hate rock climbing*. Her heart lurched.

The only way to climb up was by an ancient knotted rope that was dangling from one of the ledges. A wave of nausea hit her. Nervously, she took a bite of a small chocolate bar in her bag.

Durga started her descent, her knees shaking uncontrollably. Finally, she landed with a thud.

Thankfully, the ground was filled with shiny, soft moss that occasionally bloomed into tiny flowers in various hues.

Her eyes ached to take it all in. A thin layer of mist hung in the air, fragrant with the aroma of fruits and flowers on low branches. Sun rays filtered in, creating a gentle halo.

Durga kept walking hurriedly, running almost, excitement pounding in her ears, her fingers caressing the fresh, flower-laden, aromatic plants.

All at once, she saw a movement to the farthest corner to her left! *Am I imagining things?* she wondered, walking towards it. As she reached the spot, there was total silence. Now, she heard a soft rustle.

Intrigued, she continued in that direction. She found many, plants growing thickly together. From there, a small light was visible. Durga walked towards the light as if in a dream. Beyond the thicket was a small hut. Durga thought she even saw a small plume of smoke rising from it!

Is someone living here?

Her head felt light, and her hands trembled as she reached the hut made of straws and dried coconut leaves. The threshold was decorated with freshly drawn *muggu* (rangoli), and a small lamp twinkled beyond the door.

Durga took off her shoes and entered the house.

There was no one. In one corner, she saw a small wooden platform on which was a *grantha*, a treatise made of palm leaves.

She went down on her knees to check what was in the book.

"Oh, you won't find anything there..."

Durga staggered to the ground.

That voice. That voice belonged...to the enemy!

Durga started shivering. *Am I going mad?*

Summoning all her courage, she turned around.

It was Akanksha Raju!

Smiling. Standing in a traditional saree and adorned with Indian ornaments, looking radiant!

How can she be here? Did she have access to the same clues? Did she figure it out just as I did, now that her father is the King?

A thousand questions assailed Durga.

"I know what you are thinking...is it really me? How did I get here? How did I KNOW?" said Akanksha in her sing-song, somewhat mocking voice.

Durga nodded to all her questions.

"Well, I would say, why not?"

Durga didn't say anything.

Akanksha turned, and the diamond-studded anklets on her feet shone with a sparkle.

"Come, sit here, Durga."

"B-but you are...you are.." Durga stammered.

"The enemy...ha ha ha," laughed Akanksha.

Durga shrugged.

"Well, I wonder. I would rather say I am your best friend, actually."

Akanksha's mocking voice infuriated Durga.

"You-you have destroyed my peace."

"Really? What were you only a few months ago? A complete wimp?"

That hit her hard. Durga felt how right Akanksha was for the first time.

Akanksha drove her mad enough to work hard at improving herself. Today, she is much different from what she was only a few months ago…

Chapter Twenty

The Secret of the Poison Garden

Akanksha went to a small table-like structure on which stood an earthen pot. She dipped an ornamented silver glass into the pot, scooped some water, and offered it to Durga.

Durga, suddenly feeling parched, took the glass and drank it. The cool, aromatic water soothed her.

Shaking her head, she once again sat down.

Akanksha smiled. "So ask me."

"Ask you what? You are distracting me! I need to get out of here..."

"Really?"

"Yes. I-I need to get out here and save the-the…"

"The world?"

"Akanksha, the poison garden is a weapon!!! And in the wrong hands…" Durga was screaming.

"So that's it? Nothing else? You discerned nothing else

A well-kept secret unravels...

from the parchment?" mocked Akanksha.

"B-but there was nothing else!" said Durga as she opened her mobile phone to check the parchment picture.

Yattadagre vishameva parinaamemritopapam

tatsukham saattvikam proktamaatmabuddhiprasaadajam

"Here, Akanksha. I got it right! The meaning is — that which is like poison initially but is like nectar in its result, that joy is said to be saattvic, born of one's mental purity. See it is all about poison…," argued Durga.

Akanksha's eyes turned gentle.

"So the great Durga chose to ignore an essential clue!"

"B-but, what?" wondered Durga, still at sea.

Akanksha sighed.

"Think again. Which is like poison initially but is like nectar in its result..."

Durga went still.

"My God! Nectar? Soma! The secret of the poison garden is not poison but nectar. Nectar as in Soma!!!" shouted Durga, jumping up.

Akanksha smiled.

"Oh, Thank you! Thank you! But where is it? How can I find it? Please help me find Soma. It will help heal Janice,

Keith, and Nanna. Please," begged Durga

"What makes you think I, your sworn enemy, would help you?"

Durga looked up and saw Akanksha full in the face for the first time...

Akanksha didn't look the same. Somehow, she was different; her eyes looked kinder, and a small, bewitching smile played on her lips.

"Stop playing me, Akanksha. I need this herb..."

"Why do you need it?"

"I already told you...I need it for them!"

Akanksha's deep gaze confused Durga.

"Soma can free you of all diseases! Increase life span! So why them, when you can have it for yourself?"

"But I don't want it for myself!"

"Ha ha ha..so much pride in your values. Let me see. If I tell you the reason, you may think differently," laughed Akanksha infuriatingly.

"I am not in the habit of changing my mind," said Durga defiantly.

"Well, the water you drank just now will kill you in one hour."

"WHAT?!!! WHY...OH, WHY..." Durga stumbled

backwards.

"Why did you so unquestioningly drink the water? I, your enemy, gave you?"

"Because I TRUSTED you!"

Akanksha laughed maddeningly.

"Trust! You are funny. Now you must save yourself with the herb you know"

Durga looked up, hopefully.

"You mean I can save myself and the others?"

Akanksha went quiet for a moment and turned around dramatically.

"The herb, once plucked, must be consumed the same day. And you cannot pluck it till the next Chaitra Purnima, which comes only next year! It simply won't work. You can read in the treatise if you don't believe me."

"Is today Chaitra Purnima?" asked Durga, agonized.

Akanksha nodded.

"But I have to save Nanna, Jenny, and Keith. There may not be enough time! Akanksha, I implore you, once I pluck the herb, please take it up to the temple to save Janice and Keith. Once Janice is well, she can heal Nanna."

"What? All your lofty ideals have evaporated so soon? You are reduced to beg the enemy?"

Durga went utterly quiet.

“Nothing matters. Least of all my pride.”

“But you are prepared to die? Because of them?”

“Yes, Akanksha. Yes, I don’t mind.”

“Really? Why? Why do you want to die? If you live, you can become very powerful>”

Durga’s eyes blazed.

“No, Akanksha. I must start helping those who trusted me and sacrificed themselves for me. I cannot think about myself,” her throat went dry even as she said it.

“Noble words, Durga. But they won’t save you,” laughed Akanksha irritatingly.

Durga folded her hands in a namaskaram, tears streaming down her cheeks.

Akanksha gestured, *Come*.

Both of them walked back into the verdant gardens.

“There you are! Time is ticking. Do what you can in that time!” Akanksha’s voice rang out.

Right in the middle was a large pond filled with a profusion of water lilies in various sizes and shapes. Colorful fish were swimming in these waters as well.

“Where is it?” asked Durga as she looked back. There was no Akanksha!

She has given me the slip!

Durga checked and set her watch to a timer. Calmly, she punched out a WhatsApp message to her grandmother and her friends. It should reach them whenever the network improves, she told herself!

She circled the pond for clues, tears pouring down her cheeks. In desperation, she plonked on one of the rocks, and it made a soft musical note!

Durga jumped up. Immediately, she started touching the rows of rocks around the pond. Her guess was right; they were musical rocks. *What raga would open these? Think. Think*. She looked around for clues, but there were none.

Suddenly, she saw that the rocks were numbered in ancient Sanskrit. The one in the middle was numerical 5. Durga sang the 5th melakarta —- Manavati.

From the center of the pond, a mound rose! Right in the middle nestled a bushy plant, its leaves glistening with tiny dewdrops. A ray of the sun reflected off its leaves, giving it a golden aura.

Gathering her courage, Durga stepped on a few rocks in the pool, which seemed fairly shallow. As she neared the plant, it seemed to her that it shone even more resplendently.

Somalatha!

Her heart pounding, she carefully extracted a number of small baby saplings and leaves from the main plant and packed them into her backpack.

Now, how do I get out of here? She wondered.

As she looked around apprehensively, her foot hit a small rounded rock nestling in the grass.

When she bent down to look at it, she saw it had the Royal Seal.

Suddenly, the ground beneath her whirred and opened up, and she fell through it screaming.

In a few minutes, she came out of the vortex.

Breathing deeply, she dared to open her eyes.

Durga was in a tube-like cave facing a clear opening. Coming out, she saw the moon bridge!

Relief flooded her heart.

She ran up to the bridge.

She retraced her way back into the tunnel. This time, she didn't notice the darkness. She switched on her two powerful torches and marched on. Suddenly, the tunnel came to a halt. Looking up, she saw a panel on the ceiling, again bearing the Royal Seal. She looked at her watch. *I have 30 minutes*, she calculated. She felt around and found a lever. The panel swung open, and she heaved herself out.

"So there you are!" the low voice of Adrian sent shivers down her spine.

Durga gasped. She was back in the garbhagriha!

Adrian and Bosch stood in front of her, holding pistols. Eraka Raju and his followers were bound to the pillars.

"Hand over whatever you have picked up, and we won't kill you and your friends," growled Bosch.

Suddenly, a deep masculine voice rang out...

I know what you're thinking, punk. You are thinking, "Did he fire six shots or only five? Now, to tell you the truth, I've forgotten myself in all this excitement. But this is a .44 Magnum, the most powerful handgun in the world, and it will blow your head clean off. You've gotta ask yourself a question: 'Do I feel lucky? Well, do ya, punk?

Adrian and Bosch turned around fearfully.

Only Durga knew it was Nibbles rattling off one of Clint Eastwood's movie quotes.

In one quick movement, Durga pounced on Bosch and bit his arm. He screamed, clutching his hand, dropping his pistol. Adrian whirled around, and Durga kicked him right in his face as he fell, since it was totally unexpected.

Durga ran to Janice, crushing some leaves of Soma, and applied them to her forehead. Within seconds, she gently stirred. She did the same to Keith, who also regained consciousness. Within seconds, they were up on their feet.

In the meantime, Bosch had recovered, and so had Adrian. They stood pointing their pistols at Durga, Janice, and Keith.

It was a deadlock. A low, menacing tiger growl shattered the silence. Adrian and Bosch stared at each other in confusion.

Once again, Durga knew it was Nibbles.

Seizing the opportune moment, Durga took a small pack from her pocket, opened it, and hurled it towards Adrian and Bosch. Instinctively, they leapt into the air. As they caught it, they both gave out a blood-curdling scream and fell down unconscious within seconds.

Durga smiled. The pack had a powder made from the seeds of Abrus precatorius, which contained abrin, an extremely poisonous chemical.

"That will keep them out of action for some time," she murmured even as Janice and Keith squealed with joy. Durga revived the Akku warriors too.

Eraka Raju bowed low to Durga. "Rani Saheba, I will take care of these goons. You please leave this place now."

Suddenly, Durga glanced at her watch. *Ten seconds to death.* She glanced around to see that her backpack was lying on the ground on the other side of the hall.

"Jenny, my time's up. Tell my parents and grandmother that I love them. Akanksha is down there. Rescue her. Take care of my backpack. Take these leaves and apply to Nanna...and.." Durga fell flat on the ground.

“Diggy, Diggy, what happened to her? Keith, come here! Oh Diggy, wake up...wake up...”

Keith ran to Durga, who looked utterly unconscious. For a minute, he fell silent. Janice was sobbing. He plonked on the ground, his head in a total blur.

Suddenly, Keith got up and ran to the other side of the hall, opened the backpack, grabbed the soma leaves, crushed them, and applied them to Durga.

Durga trembled and sat up, looking groggy!

“Thank goodness,” wept Janice. Keith smiled, relief flooding his heart.

“Wh-what happened, guys?” Durga got up and looked questioningly at her friends. They looked at her happily.

“Akanksha...she was down there, you know,” murmured Durga.

Keith and Janice gaped.

“Akanksha??? Sh-she er, she is fine,” They both looked at each other, deciding not to say anything at this moment to Durga.

“You mean, you guys rescued her too! Thank God!”

“D, let’s get out,” said Keith. Janice stood up and started walking out. Durga followed.

Slowly, Durga, Keith, and Janice made their way out of the temple. It was nearly dusk.

The minute they got out, they stood transfixed to the spot!

Queen Mother and Durga's mother, Professor Jaywant, Abhik, black cat commandos from the Indian Army, and police personnel had just reached the temple premises. *They got my message!* Durga ran to her mother and grandmother and hugged them.

Durga woke up refreshed. The events of yesterday seemed like a dream. The nagging feeling of sadness that had haunted her for weeks had subsided. They were all back at the Devdi. The Gajendrapatiraju family helicopter and another one from the Indian Army helped them all get back.

The first thing that Durga did on arriving at the Devdi was to revive her father with the Soma leaves. His memory came back! Immediately, Queen Mother commanded Dhyaneshwara Raju and his family to return to their home. They reluctantly obliged, having realized that Dr. Harish was now fully recovered.

Durga jumped out of bed and got ready within minutes, wearing her best Indian outfit for the ceremonial breakfast.

She stepped out to see her friends. They all group-hugged.

The minute she walked into the corridor, her father, who had also come out of his room at the same time, stopped and embraced her.

Durga was so happy to see that her father was fully recovered.

"Nanna, I have a few questions."

"Yes, Amma, ask away."

"A curious thing. It was Akanksha Raju who helped when I was down there. She was in a hut, wearing jewels and provoking me. She did lead me to the herb. Now that she knows, does this mean it will become common knowledge? I mean, her father did become the King temporarily. So, will any other family members know about the secret, too? Isn't it dangerous?"

Dr. Harish Varma came to a standstill and stared at Durga for a moment.

Durga looked confused and smiled questioningly.

"Amma, let's sit here for a few minutes," offered her father, sitting on a small ornamental bench. Durga slid beside him. Dr. Varma gestured for the others to carry on. They obliged immediately.

"What happened down there? Can you narrate the whole experience without missing any details?"

Durga did. Her father listened attentively, his facial expressions changing rapidly from wonder to surprise to amazement!

Dr. Varma sighed and was silent for a few moments, after she finished.

“Amma, I had only cracked half the riddle when I wrote you that letter. Moreover, I knew I was being followed, so I didn’t complete the trail. Then there was the accident...”

Durga shuddered.

“Nanna, was it really an accident?”

Dr. Varma paused.

“I don’t know, Amma. I can’t remember! But leave that now. I am so proud of you. You cracked the secret of the Poison Garden and found Soma! You have displayed not only an analytical approach but also empathy and kindness, of which I am more proud!”

Durga smiled rapturously.

“Your grandfather, the King, said this quest would test the character in many ways! Now I realize what he was saying!”

Both sat silently for a few moments.

“What must have happened there is probably this. I am only guessing this. Following some ancient texts and comparing them with plant candidates, there are theories that coming in contact with certain kinds of Soma could induce hallucinations. These may have been planted there to confuse any intruders. You might have brushed against or come into contact with some of those, which explains the visions.”

Durga looked at her dad incredulously.

"I don't think so. I mean, she practically led me to Soma, Nanna! How could that be if she was a mere vision?"

Her father smiled.

"The clue might have been in your inner consciousness that the vision may have triggered. I am still guessing here…"

Durga nodded thoughtfully. *Maybe some mysteries remain that!*

Chapter 21

Green Allegiants

Breakfast was a cozy affair, noisy, cheerful, and brimming with happiness. After breakfast, Durga's parents sat next to the Queen Mother. Soon after, Durga, Janice, Keith, and Abhik joined them in the room.

As they settled down, her grandmother spoke.

"First and foremost, my blessings to my son, the King, my beloved daughter-in-law Lakshmi, and my granddaughter Durga. I am happy that Durga, with valuable help from her friends, solved an ancient mystery. I would like my son to speak now."

A hush settled as Dr. Harish Varma started to speak.

"My congratulations to the brave little warriors sitting here. What is astonishing is that you have not hesitated despite all the risks involved. It's very inspiring. It must have been an exciting journey of mind-boggling discoveries. And indeed, the journey would have tested your resolve, imagination, and determination. You have collectively discovered a real treasure of ancient plant resources, which I am sure would prove very valuable. These plant resources hold the key to the future. The future of this planet."

"Sir, how can we stop plant theft? People like Adrian seem so professional!" asked Keith.

"Yes, my dear Keith. It's a battle we must continue to fight. This is not just one country's problem but a global one."

"Do you think Dr. Uwe was attacked on our school grounds, Nanna?" asked Durga.

"Oh, it is rather hard to guess at this point. He was hoping to meet Kenny that day to hand over the envelope with the Begonia Tessaricarpa sapling, and the message to find Adrian Gerber. He also tried to warn me about the possible theft at the rose show. It's a fact that he was extremely allergic to Aconitum. He may have stumbled into the bush accidentally, or associates of Adrian may have shoved him. Dr. Uwe was onto Adrian for some time. It's a tragedy that we lost him," explained Dr. Varma sadly.

There was a moment's silence around the table.

"Nanna, I am curious that Dr. Pinnasetty falsely identified Begonia Tessaricarpa. Now, why would he do that? Also, I remember seeing Dr. Uwe's Mickey Mouse watch on the table. I know it was his because it was I who identified his body on the school grounds. Is he somehow connected to all this?"

Dr. Harish Varma paused thoughtfully.

"Well, I don't think he could be connected in any way to this business. I mustn't say this in front of you guys, but he's not very talented. So, he might easily have made that mistake. Now, as for the Mickey Mouse watch, it could have been a sheer coincidence since there is nothing to connect him with this plant theft business. He lives simply, like a typical Government employee. He doesn't even own a car. No. I don't think he has any major ambitions."

Durga was silent. She was sure he was somehow connected. *I will need to dig a bit deeper.*

"Well, bravehearts like Dr. Uwe must become our inspiration. We must make sufficient efforts to preserve the immense resources we already possess. Each of us is responsible for this. The West is ahead of us in this concept. They established Gene Banks even before World War II. These gene banks have been collecting, multiplying, and distributing seeds for breeding and research for over five decades. You may have heard about the Svalbard Global Seed Vault facility in the Arctic. The vault has been carved inside a mountain mass that has permafrost, with a temperature of minus 3-4 degrees Celsius.

India has a similar facility — the Indian Seed Vault at Chang La, in the Himalayan region of Ladakh."

Dr. Varma paused and smiled as he saw all of them were listening with rapt attention.

"I have created a private facility in the Himalayas with the same conditions, so whatever samples Adrian had stolen are in there. Safe!"

"Wow!" "Great!" "Thank God!" Durga and her friends reacted.

"Here, we can store our samples safely. Especially the poisonous ones, so that no one can get their hands on them."

"What is the secret of Somalatha, Nanna? How can it have medicinal properties only for a single day?" asked Durga.

"I don't know, Amma. Science still cannot explain this kind of anomalous phenomenon in the plant kingdom. Maybe with sufficient research, we may crack this mystery. Our civilization in India has unraveled many such astounding discoveries. This herb Somalatha, with its extraordinary healing properties, needs to be researched further. It has immense potential. It could be that Chaitra Purnima is the day when the herb realizes its potential, possibly because of external weather conditions or other abiotic factors. My team and I shall start working on it."

"The parchment we found indicates a lot more, Nanna."

"As I said before, I managed to crack only half the puzzle. Unfortunately, my father, the King, had passed by the time I could retrieve the details. Now that we have all witnessed your ingenuity, I feel I can confidently relinquish the task of solving the mysteries to you, Durga, and to your dear friends. Today, I miss my dearest friend Kenny, who has completely missed all the excitement!"

Suddenly, a man walked into the hall. “That man, that man!” screamed Durga. All of them looked at him astounded.

Laughing, the man took off his wig. It was Dr. Kennedy Chandrasekhar!

“Dad!” squealed Janice as she enveloped him in a bear hug. Dr. Chandrasekhar laughed.

Durga was spellbound. “So it was you, Uncle Kenny! You were the injured person on the school grounds? Why this disguise?”

“Your father gave me all the instructions in advance. In any case, too many people were watching you and us. I wanted to be discreet and guide you along the way. You know how much I love playing Sherlock Holmes.”

“Did you send the twig and the letter too?”

“Yes. I did.”

All of them clapped.

“I think it’s time Durga spoke,” said Queen Mother, her eyes twinkling.

“Thank you, Bamma. First, I would like you to give a rousing applause to Nibbles, who saved the day literally,” said Durga, smiling.

Everyone applauded. Nibbles squealed happily.

“This year is...oh, what can I say?… It has been super, super exciting! I learnt so much! First and foremost, thank you, Nanna and Amma. It's all because of those expeditions you took me on that I could do it all so easily. And thanks to Bamma and Uncle Kenny for protecting me. My BFFs Janice, Keith, Abhik, and Nibbles for egging me to try new things all along, even though I was being my usual reluctant self," Durga couldn't control her giggles. Then she turned solemn.

"The election, the campaigning. Then, oh God! the detention was fantastic. Because we could help people who needed it. The quest, the dangerous quest. Not even once did you guys hesitate. You were with me all along to the extent of nearly getting killed!" Durga stopped and looked at Janice and Keith. Her eyes were glistening.

"Even Eraka Raju and his warriors who almost died saving us. Finally, Akanksha Raju, my enemy who made me realize my true potential. I am reminded of that quote in the parchment that I read so many times over the last few months." Saying this, Durga took out her mobile and read it aloud.

Yattadagre vishameva parinaamemritopapam

tatsukham saattvikam proktamaatmabuddhiprasaadajam

"That which is like poison initially but is like nectar in its result. I overcame my inhibitions, just like the sloka mentions. Just as Uncle, I mean Captain Arun Sharma, from the Old Age Home, said, I would. I have all of you to thank!"

A great silence fell across the room, followed by thunderous applause.

"Bravo!"

"Well said!"

Janice, Keith, and Abhik came towards her for a noisy high-five.

"Ahem," Abhik cleared his throat.

"May I say something?"

"Yes, yes," chorused everyone.

"It was stupendous seeing our Durga transform! Her instincts and leadership were superlative and led us all the way. Cheers, Diggy!"

Durga went pink.

"Yeah, yeah!"

Durga turned to her grandmother "Bamma, where is Mr. Krishna Murthy? Er, he...I mean he..."

"I know, Amma. I found out. Anyways, he's missing. The police now attribute Pushpa's murder to him. We now have a new manager."

"And Adrian and Bosch? "

"No sign of them. They seem to have disappeared," said her grandmother.

"I wanted to meet and thank Eraka Raju and his warriors!" said Durga ruefully.

"Here I am, Princess."

They whirled around to see Eraka Raju bowing low before Durga.

"Akku is at your service. Allow us to guard you. You need protection. There are still evil people around," said Eraka Raju humbly.

"Yes, Diggy. I believe he's right," pressed Janice.

"You must trust Akku. They will be there to protect you. Don't underestimate their potential," said her father.

Durga was silent for a while and then nodded in agreement.

"What happens to the temple?"

"The temple is sealed. Akku will protect the temple as always. It is, however, now directly under our control. We have applied to the Government of India to grant us guardianship of the land and the temple as a Corporate Social Responsibility project. The Prime Minister has agreed and asked us to take care of these precious resources," said Queen Mother.

"Dhyaneshwara Raju and the verdict, Amma? Now that Nanna is well…."

"Ah, yes. The minute your father recovered, we filed a

counter for the previous verdict, which will undoubtedly be resolved in your father's favor. We also found a copy of your grandfather's will. Your father is now officially the King, and you are a Princess," said Durga's mother, smiling.

"Amma, your lawyer prowess is at work again," said Durga admiringly. Her mom smiled.

"It's teamwork, folks," said Dr. Kennedy Chandrasekhar.

"Yes, yes."

Durga, Durga, I will get you yet, the Professor raged. But silently.

His anger shook him up, and he felt drained out, almost like there was no breath left in him. Still, he could not show such emotion.

The Professor was not a brutal man and had been self-controlled all his life, at least outwardly.

But he hated Dr. Varma with almost murderous violence. And now Durga, too.

He shook his head.

Though he was dining with a beautiful lady this evening at the well-respected Club del Doge restaurant of the luxurious Gritti Palace in Venice, the food was tasteless in his mouth. The chef had assured them that the dishes were made with fresh ingredients from the Rialto Market.

The Gritti Palace is a former noble residence on Venice's Grand Canal that boasts exceptional Santa Maria Delle Salute Church views and splendid rooms filled with antiques and Murano glass. The evening was tranquil. A gentle breeze blew across his face. Somewhere in the distance, he could hear the cries of retreating seagulls.

The lady opposite him, dressed in an antique mini-train sheath Dior dress with aquatic patterns in silver, cream, and translucent shades, looked entrancing.

She's lovely but dumb.

Even after Adrian called him, he calmly walked from La Fenice Opera House, 500 meters from St. Mark's Square, to the Hotel. The Vaporetto water bus stop at Santa Maria del Giglio was 400 meters away. He would take one of those to get back.

The money was not a big concern, even at this point, thanks to all the stolen plant resources he had sold over the years. His thirst was to find that exceptional one like Somalatha. That would be his jackpot!

His only hope at this point was that Adrian had confirmed that there were some biological samples in Durga's backpack.

It was only a matter of time. He would track her every move from now on.

He was sure Durga would not stop. Nor would Dr. Varma.

The Professor sighed. At this rate, my masquerade as the moronic Dr. Pinnasetty will need to continue.

Two weeks later. On a sunny afternoon.

Durga, Janice, Abhik and Keith were sitting on the lawn having tea. Butterflies were buzzing; fragrant roses were in full bloom.

Creamy scones, tea cakes, an assortment of pastries, freshly baked doughnuts, mirchi bajjis, milkshakes — there was an unending selection before them.

"Guys, remember, a part of our challenge is deciphering the parchment."

"Sure, D! To another Fountain of youth and that sort of thing?" Abhik's eyes were already twinkling with excitement. He simply loved the Pirates series.

"Hey relax guys…We have only just come back; we should rest now. I mean, this literally, figuratively, metaphysically..." Janice drawled.

Nibbles squealed in delight.

"You want to stay back, Jenny?" teased Durga.

"Heyyyyyaa!" scowled Janice.

Durga smiled.

"You know I have been thinking about it. There are so many issues concerning biodiversity and its conservation. We must do something about it."

"Like what?" asked Keith, Abhik, and Janice together.

Just then, Suma approached their table and announced that Queen Mother wished to see them in her chamber.

Queen Mother greeted them with a smile and motioned them to sit. They nodded and settled into comfortably stuffed antique chairs.

"News travels fast. You know someone has already heard about your exploits," said Queen Mother mysteriously.

They waited.

"It seems you have an assignment!"

Queen Mother's eyes twinkled.

"What?"

"Assignment?"

"What is it about?"

"Who?"

Four voices rang out in unison.

Queen Mother held up her hand.

"Hold on. Durga, here you are. A letter from the Royal

Family of Bhutan. I understand they have a 'plant' problem you can solve. With help from your friends."

Durga eagerly took the letter from her grandmother's hand.

The letter emblazoned with the royal insignia of Bhutan was addressed to her!

Your Royal Highness Princess Durgavathi,

Greetings.

I learned of your prowess in identifying germplasm from Dr. Kennedy Chandrasekhar, whom I had the fortune of meeting at the Biodiversity Conference at Cambridge. You have undoubtedly inherited this great talent from your father, His Imperial Highness Dr. Harish Varma.

This secret lies in Bhutan's Taktsang Palphug Monastery, also known as Paro Taktsang or Tiger's Nest Monastery.

I have requested Her Majesty the Queen to permit your travel to Bhutan.

I will explain everything to you when we meet.

We will wait for your arrival at the earliest.

Signed

"Why me? I mean us? Now that Nanna is all well?" asked Durga.

“Because you have the advantage of being slightly more inconspicuous than me!” teased Dr. Varma with a smile.

Durga, Keith, Abhik, and Janice went speechless for a full minute.

“Bhutan!”

“Aiyeee!”

“I love it. Let’s go.”

“Stop. Not so fast. This can happen only during your holidays after your exams.”

The gentle voice of Queen Mother cut through the clamor.

“Awww, okay, Bamma.”

Once they were alone, Durga started to pace up and down.

“What is it D,” asked Keith.

“You know, we are involved in this wonderful quest of identifying lost plant species, germplasm, solving riddles, and all that. We should call ourselves something.”

“What do you mean?”

“I don’t know. Like Famous Five or..”

“Or Secret Seven. C’mon, it’s childish,” laughed Janice.

“No, it could be much more serious. We could be known

as a group that goes on adventures and solves mysteries relating to the plant kingdom. I quite like the idea," said Abhik.

"We call ourselves by a name that denotes that we strive towards this cause," said Durga slowly.

"What would our name be then?" asked Janice.

"I already have it," smirked Abhik.

"Abhi, what is it?" they chorused.

"Hmm...how about the Green Liege?"

Durga and Janice looked thoughtful.

"Liege is good...only that it sounds warrior-like."

"I thought you would like it, D," murmured Abhik.

"But...I was thinking more like...allegiance..." said Durga slowly.

"You mean the Green Allegiance?"

"That's it! How about Green Allegiants?"

"Yes, Diggy, perfect!" Keith exclaimed.

Green Allegiants! shrieked Nibbles.

A month later.

"So the infamous APJs are back in action. Well, get back to your rooms! You know I am the Head Girl now!" the jeering voice of Akanksha Raju greeted them as they entered their dorms. Jagannath Mishra and Elizabeth Waltham greeted them with a tiny smile when Akanksha was not watching.

Durga, Janice, Keith, and Abhik grinned.

"Yo Sugar Candy Head Girl, don't forget we won the House Cup. Your Instagram tactics didn't work there!" sneered Janice.

"Humph! So what? I won, and you lost. And about that House Cup…there is always this year. We will get you yet," shouted Akanksha, walking away.

"She is just super jealous that we won. Thanks to extra points from our detention activities and excellent herbariums," chuckled Keith.

Akku had helped them to assemble their herbariums, and they were so exceptional, that Professor Anantnarayan had them exhibited in the foyer of their labs, in a glass case.

"*Always the dullness of fools is the whetstone of the wits*," quoted Keith.

"Shakespeare. *As you like it,*" rattled off Janice proudly.

"Good for you, Jen!" Keith exclaimed.

"Ah, that tone of surprise. Why, may I ask?"

"Alright, alright…You both. Cut it out. What does it mean anyway?" asked Durga.

"A whetstone is something used to sharpen a knife. So the fact that a fool is 'dull' helps the witty person to become more 'sharp' or smart than he was before," explained Keith.

"Yes. I agree! Thanks to Akanksha, I realized my potential!" said Durga.

"And thanks to Keith, I looked up Shakespeare," grinned Janice.

"Heeyyyyy!"

"Guys, time to raise a toast! Here's to Green Allegiants!!"

Campai! Cheers! Salud! screamed Nibbles as the Green Allegiants clinked glasses of fresh lime soda.

The Sun set in the distance.

THE END

Acknowledgments

I extend my heartfelt gratitude to those who have played pivotal roles in shaping both my life and this book:

Dr. U Prasada Rao, my father, who sowed the seeds of a profound love for plants in my heart, nurturing a lifelong passion.

Mrs. U Satya Sri, my mother, whose boundless love for books and the art of writing inspired me to explore the world of storytelling.

Ramakanth Thumrugoti, my husband, steadfast pillar of strength and unwavering companion, who stands by me through every challenge and triumph of my creative journey.

Manonmani Thumrugoti, my beloved daughter, who constantly helps me see the wonders of life through a special lens.

Umakanth Thumrugoti, my brother-in-law who patiently read my working draft and suggested valuable insights.

Priya Gazdar, my friend, for the editing and the fresh perspective she added to the script.

Aruna Bashakarla, Padma Ravi Kumar, and Team RBC Worldwide whose creative prowess played an instrumental role in bringing this book to life, shaping its design, and ensuring its visual appeal.

Special thanks to my Managers at East-West Seed - Dilip Rajan, Maaike Groot, and GC Shivakumar for their support and encouragement.

ANANDA THUMRUGOTI

Ananda Thumrugoti loves to weave stories, especially about plants and nature. She realized these could make great themes for young readers. Now, she writes stories that mix adventure and mystery with botanical twists. It's her way of creating awareness and excitement about the plant kingdom. Ananda is the Head of Corporate Communications and Media Relations at East-West Seed India, where she continues to blend her professional expertise with her passions, fostering a greater understanding and appreciation for agriculture and the environment.